The Day the Sun Shed Bloody Tears

The Day the Sun Shed *Bloody* Tears

MIYA DAVIDS

iUniverse, Inc.
New York   Bloomington

The Day the Sun Shed Bloody Tears

iUniverse books may be ordered through booksellers or by contacting:

iUniverse
1663 Liberty Drive
Bloomington, IN 47403
www.iuniverse.com
1-800-Authors (1-800-288-4677)

ISBN: 978-1-4502-2957-9 (sc)
ISBN: 978-1-4502-2959-3 (ebk)

Printed in the United States of America

iUniverse rev. date: 05/04/2010

I present this story in honor of the World War II victims, and my heartfelt tribute to all whom perished.

Sincerely
Miya Davids: Author

Table of Contents

Chapter 1: Memory

I hear sound of the planes in a distance, *"An air raid?"* I shouted run for the shelter. But my body would not budge; and I stood as if a statue, falling bombs exploding all around me as the ground shook as if violent an earth-quacks. Standing in amidst of walls of roaring fire, helplessly I watched the burning estate, *"Somebody I am on fire ... Help!"* I screamed, but my voice was locked in nightmare, holding me in captive, and my body was stone statue ...

I awoke being totally exhausted, as I lay motionless, and I have mustered tad amount of remaining strength to pull myself up, walking out on the verandah. Breading in a cool jasmine scented crisp air, attempt to shake off the shroud of haunting nightmare.

Perfume of jasmine sedates my mind, as I cast eyes on velvet black sky splashed with stars, shooting bright twinkling lights, reminds me of holding the baby Miss Tami on my lap, watching stars just like tonight with my Mistress Shizuka many years ago.

Suddenly out of clear, *"What if ... my life would end tomorrow, or the next minute in the blink of an eye?"* An assault of rude awakening shattered my serene moment; as if a bolt of lightning struck thrust a blade of an inevitable life's fate.

Until this moment, I have regarded my life for a granted, just as same as the never-ending ticking sounds of clock. But hastened by an urgent reality of life, I have immediately begun to chronicle my extraordinary life story, spanned over four decades.

At the height of WWII Japan was defeated at an every turn, and the reserved means to counter attack powerful United States military was exhausted unable to combat the assaults. One such day, surprise an air raid has left our remote farming village in burnt ruin, thus the world as I knew has changed from that moment on. I was twenty-eight years old then.

My younger sister Yumi and I have survived the fire, but left without a master, and Miss Tami, an only survivor of the family, was orphaned at the young age of thirteen.

Without a choice three of us found ourselves in a pit of refugees' hell, just as so many others. Luckily I was young and had strength to care for my sister and Miss Tami, I picked wild vegetation to provide them with the food. And then I remembered about going to the seashore, as a small child parent sent me to gather clams for the family meal, when tides were low, and Yumi and I had to climb down the steep hill to the spot on shore where clams were.

I still remember we brought back a bucket full of clams for mother, and she cooked them over the fire.

In an era I was born, newborn female infant was killed at birth for a reason of family was too poor to feed another mouth, it was openly accepted though discreetly practiced deed, however, male infant was spared of death for two reasons. The boy child has a pretty face; he will be sold as a child prostitute and when he is able to pick up the shovel, his parents put him to work in a field.

I have two older brothers, but they considered female was inferior gender; and they have neither cared about me nor acknowledged as their sister, but I had to obey and serve whatever their needs were.

Moreover, my father has ignored me; he never spoke to me even we were working side by side in the small family field. Growing up, I often wondered the reason of my being spared of death, but I sensed my father would sell me to prostitution at a first chance, to get his hand on the large sum of money.

I was six years old when my sister Yumi was born, and she was as delicate as a beautiful flower, too frail to pick up a heavy shovel to work in field, so I did her share of work to shield her from Father's wrath, and I suspected my father would sell her to prostitution, no matter of her an age; his only thought was on a windfall of money.

I have been spared of death to be sold as a prostitute? A thought haunted throughout my growing years. My mother knew what was in my future, but she could not voice her protest against her husband, and she lived with a sad heart.

"My precious Taka, you are only five years old; I wish I could give you a doll to play with instead of having you work as a farmhand. My poor child." Mother said, I watched wiping tears with her coarse knobby hand, and she hugged me when we were alone, an imprint of memories I carried in my heart all my life.

We were dirt poor, and parents had no money to repair the house, even though the farmhouse was in disrepair, but in spite of ran down farmhouse, I thank our good fortune for provided us with shelter, not have to live as if field rodents.

We lived in a sparsely populated farming village, approximately seventy-two miles west of the big city of Fukuoka, which encompassed large foreign and domestic businesses, oil refineries, coalmines, steel mills; as well as an international seaport, and many small businesses.

When I was fifteen and Yumi was nine years old, all my years of haunting suspicions were proven true. A stranger came to the house riding on a rickshaw, and two big bodyguards guarding him; apparently he was a very rich man to afford expensive silk garments and looked well fed. But a sight of him horrified me, and my intuition told me who he was and why he came, because I have heard so much about this man from the farm girls at the village's water wall.

I felt chill, realizing the man had to be the owner of prostitution house in the big city, and he came to buy Yumi and me. In fear I ran out from house taking my sister Yumi, who was more frightened by my unusual behavior than not knowing what was happening. Holding Yumi's small hand tight I walked fast to hurry, before my father finds us gone, Yumi had nearly running to keep up the paces with me, as we headed for the Araki estate.

I was praying and counting on the senior Araki to help us, I heard he has always rendered an aide to poor people, when I go to fetch a bucket of water, and the girls talked about him as if he was their savior. Although the Araki estate was only one kilometer away 2.7 miles, but I felt Yumi and I was running to an end of the world.

I believed karma has led us right to the wealthy Araki family, and luckily, instead of turning us away, the senior Araki took pity on us when I told him about we were being sold us prostitutes, to the owner of prostitution house. Senior Araki listened to my tale of woe, rescued us from lifetime of sex slavery and gave us the opportunity to work as servants, from that moment forward Yumi and my life has changed.

Then the war began and the entire population had plunge into a cauldron of hell, churning with the bitter taste of hunger and poverty with no way out.

Three of us survived fire, but my being an oldest I was the surrogate mother to care for the orphaned Miss Tami and my sister Yumi, desperately to survive everyday a day at a time. I hung on to my sliver of human dignity, held onto my belief of our future is alive and well. This is my testimony of how I led three of us through WWII chaos.

Chapter 2: Axis of Avarice

At the far western edge of the Pacific Ocean, the series of islands called Japan lie in a bow shape, separated from the Asian continent by the Sea of Japan, in line from the USSR south to the East China Sea. In 1937, Japan won the war over the USSR and after enduring decades of war. Finally the peace prevailed over Japanese people, and confirming their belief of Japan was the most powerful country, more importantly no longer the citizens were war weary, and they have jubilantly rejoiced the victory, believing the sun arises and sets over the Japan, proudly held their white cloth flag with a red circle in the center which to symbolized the Rising Sun.

For a first time in many years all was well, and, people have welcomed tomorrow with a glad tiding enjoyed their daily life, never a vision of threat of another war would occur in their near future, the thoughts never entered their mind.

Japan is small string of mountainous islands, only an eleven percent of real estate available for housing, roads, factories and institutional buildings etc ... More to the point of an importance, the farming fields were at a premium; unable to produce and provide the essential commodities most of them were imported, and adding to the problem, Japanese population was growing at an alarming pace.

I was a naïve young girl when the WWII started, and the General Hideki Tojo was the prime minister of Japan, however, he was oblivious to an ominous dark shroud already rising in the horizon, initiated an invasion of Korea through China to gain needed real estate; his attempt to eradicate the out-of-control population problem, thus many Japanese has immigrated to Korea and China.

The Imperial Japanese Army has penetrated deep into China's interior, confiscated goods Japan could not produce, and all those dire need commodities were sent to the homeland.

Emboldened by his successes, General Tojo sent the Imperial Army to infiltrate into the South Pacific islands and commandeered raw materials Japan was unable to produce, such as rubber, crude oil, sugar, and many other goods. However, as a token of gratitude, General Tojo has accolade the islanders as subsidiaries of honorable Japan and having that excuse, freely encroached upon the territory to confiscate the abundances of products to be sent to Japan.

"He is our great leader." Citizens have praised the General, his effort in supplying abundances of commodity good to be available, for the public, which were none existent. To show their gratitude for the General Tojo, the grateful citizens hung his portrait just as big next to the Emperors in the entire household. General Tojo's ego and the axis of avarice grew; and having no obstacles in his path, continued to invade even more of the Pacific islands, using natives to work as a labor, allowing them to keep a small portion of harvested good not enough to sustain their family, which alarmed the United States.

Japanese representatives were summoned to America for a joint negotiation, in an attempt to end Japan's brazen encroachment on the Pacific islands. However, General Tojo believed he was a second coming of the legendary warlord, Tokugawa, defied the ongoing peace negotiations and secretly plotting to attack the Pearl Harbor.

The Hawaiian Islands were strategically positioned in the middle of the Pacific Ocean; and possessing Hawaiian Islands under his dominion were Tojo's dream, and he knew to gain an ultimate power to rule the world, thus attacking the United States and the western and eastern hemisphere would be a fail-proof, and he could successfully gain insurmountable riches and the power. General Tojo could not resist the irresistible possibilities; and the thoughts enticed him at every waking moment.

On Sunday, December the seventh, 1941, the Imperial command navy pilots have stealthily deployed to attack Pearl Harbor; destroying U.S. Navy battleships were on peacetime duty, inflicted insurmountable casualties and damages, consequently provoking a mighty anger of the gentle giant, the United States.

"Great Success! Mission accomplished." The headline was splashed boldly across the front page of newspapers, relaying the detailed accounts of how the surprise attack on Pearl Harbor was successfully accomplished, and the entire country of Japan celebrated as though they have won the war; however, a crucial factor has been omitted from published accounts.

The squadron of Imperial pilots had to bypass the U.S. oil storage facilities intact, the consequence of lacking fuel for the return flight. This fact has been codified thus: Consequence of the low fuel, squadron has bypassed the valuable U.S. maintenance facilities and oil storage area, left its entire U.S. oil reserve, negating further assault on the Hawaiian Island. The dereliction

The war progressed, but the news released truth, people have celebrated the victors' grand

allowed the U.S. Navy to recover and launch an immediate full-force military operation to counterattack Japan. Moreover, out of harm's way, there were Lexington, Enterprise, and Hornet task forces at sea, ferrying aircraft to Wake and Midway Islands.

On December the eighth, 1941 a day after the surprise attack on Pearl Harbor, America has declared war against Japan by the United States Congress's unanimous approval; however, hyped up Japanese people believed they will win the war, sent their son, husband, and father off to the war gave an extravagant send off party, as if to the celebration of holiday.

Two months after Pearl Harbor was attacked, the American general Doolittle has strategically deployed the mother ship USS Hornet, carrying the specially modified B-25 bomber, to a point of coordinate in the Pacific Ocean. From this point, attacking the Japanese homeland was possible, and the first target was the Tokyo, Japan's capital.

From that moment on, the tide has turned against Japan, but the Japanese people closed their eyes, even the enemy's attack was at their front door, and they celebrated an erroneous preconceived victory, proclaiming they were the unbeatable superior race on earth. The banners boasting propaganda stating,

Never fear. We are the mighty power, were posted everywhere to pacify the Japanese people.

Ironically, however, in a admits of shrouding ominous war clouds, the emperor did not have a clue as to the changing world outside of his palace, your highness was concealed from any disturbing news. The palace where emperor resides was in the center of Tokyo, surrounded by a wide and deep moat, accessible only by a single double-arched bridge, so the Emperor remained incognizant to the current crisis, still conversed in an ancient language that has exists only in the history books. Unaware of the war cloud shrouding over Japan, the Emperor has decided to tour his country, for the first time in the history of the monarchy he left the sanctuary of his palace with only few of his guards.

The citizens rejoiced, when news of the Emperor's visit was made public, proclaiming, *"Our living Shinto god, the Emperor is coming."*

People came walking from every surrounding town and village, lining an each side of the street from before dawn, forming a wall of people holding flags in their hands, not wanting to miss the once-in-a-lifetime opportunity of seeing their living god in person. I had walk distances carrying Miss Tami on a piggyback to see the event.

The hours passed as more people kept arriving, packing each side of the street as the heat of the day became intolerable. Suddenly, a thunderous shout of *"Banzai"* broke out, signaling the approaching Emperor's motorcade, and in a mere moment his motorcade sped past in front of them, leaving them with only glimpse of the living Sinto god. Although it was only flash of a moment, people were able to capture an extraordinary vivid image of the Emperor in their minds.

The Emperor was a direct descendant of the legendary Sun Goddess. Amaterasu, who created Japan, he wore a traditional uniform of coal black suit and a billed black cap with a white feather. Strands of gold braid draped across his chest, gold tassels hung from his epaulets, and the gold buttons on his suit shone under the midday sun, casting a brilliant contrast against his black suit, waved his glistening white-gloved hand to line of his subjects. Ironically, the Emperor did not have a clue as to the relevancy between himself and the suffering poverty of his people.

The war progressed, but the news released was contrary to the truth, people have celebrated the victors' grandeur, adding yet more of erroneous belief of already inflated an ego. The children were brainwashed to believe they were the descendants of the Shinto God, thus the Emperor was their Father, the living God.

The huge VICTORY banners were displayed everywhere to pacify the public, boasting, *"Never fear, enemies wouldn't dare attempt to harm the god's children."* War songs were sung to heighten the already crazed war hype, while all other songs were banned. English words were eliminated from school textbooks, numbers were written in Japanese characters. Math symbols and science formulas were also replaced with Japanese characters, which created confusion among the students.

The boy students wore camouflaged battle khakis, instead of a traditional black suit school uniforms, and a white bandanna bearing a red circle in the center replaced the regulation black billed cap. Girls wore Monpe, baggy trousers, which all females had to wear, we made it with taking a part of kimono, and the students dismember their pleated black uniform skirts.

One pair of black canvas shoes was available, by a lottery every three to four months, for a class of thirty-five pupils. Necessary staples were sent to the war front, and the public had to make do with what was left. Goods were rationed monthly with coupons, but a month's portion of rice has lasted only three days, so people raided fields, or in desperation ate whatever they can find.

Wives, mothers, and daughters has made good luck scarves for their men, stood on street corners, in front of a store, and at the train station asking passersby to sew a single knot with red thread onto a white scarf, and many people have willingly stitched in a single knot. Every day in school, scarves were passed in class among the students to sew a knot, and each student secured a stitch with their prayers for a man they will never meet. Also at the boys' school, they too were asked to sew a stitch; however, some of the boy students needed help from a teacher to stitch a knot. After one thousand knots had been sewn, the scarf was sent to someone's husband, father, or the son.

The government's attempt to replenish the war chest, more tax were imposed on citizens who were already heavily laden with taxes, and for them to pay for it, people had to sell the last of their family heirlooms; farmers sold essential survival tools and the farm animals. Furthermore, it was mandatory order for the citizens to remove the gold and silver caps from their teeth to be donated, but all those efforts yielded only a drop in the bucket to supplement the cost of war.

Inevitably, one by one all of the Pacific territories Japan has seized were lost to the United States through perilous battles. Not only loosing the territories, but also many lives, battleships, and the planes, until there were no more replacements available. Thus Japan's prized Zero fighter planes were built in part with plywood and cardboard.

Young students were inducted into the Imperial Army; only the frail and sick escaped the obligatory mandate. However, sick and an old had to work in the factories and farms, if they can stand on their two feet, and women and children have worked to maintain the labor forces. Students collected pine tar to supplement the fuel source; they stayed in the woods, keep working until they met their day's quota, even after the nightfall.

Chapter 3: Araki Legacy

My host family Araki has owned a flourishing real estate business for generations, and they lived in southern Kyushu Island. Currently the senior Araki, age seventy-three, was the head of the real estate business, he was tall, impressive man, unlike many physically small Oriental men: His pure white hair and a striking chiseled and tanned face, resembled a handsome Greek man, and he was still sprite enough to put in a full day of work with his son Kenji, an executive, younger version of his father.

Kenji and his wife Shizuka had four sons, all grown and as tall as their father. They were the junior executives, but the youngest son has attended the University of California, majored in business management. In the postwar economy, the Araki real estate business prospered with a cornucopia of successes, and their wealth had grown to astronomical heights. Life was grand—no one envisioned the doom of another war waiting in his and her future. But inevitably, the Araki family will be claimed by the fate.

The family's day has begun with Grandfather performing the prayer ritual in the altar room of the Buddhist shrine located in the center of the courtyard. But this morning, Mistress Shizuka felt ill and excused herself from attending the Morning Prayer, and sat on her favorite settee on the verandah to subdue her disquiet, submerged in a tranquil solitude and enjoying the drifting perfume of jasmine, carried by a soft breeze, as she gazed towards a slowly curved sliver of silver line, which merged with the cobalt Pacific, on the never-ending panoramic horizon in a distant.

A physician was summoned to examine Mistress Shizuka, and the result of his finding was surprise to Grandfather and Kenji. According to physician, Mistress was two months into pregnancy, but she was past childbearing age and pregnancy this late in her life was not welcomed. After the shock wore off, both men were jubilant, and they hurried to see their Mistress, who will be happy with prospect of having another child. But they found the Mistress was in a somber mood, and her unseeing eyes were fixed on something only she could see, while I groomed her tresses.

"Shizuka my dear, Father and I are beside ourselves with joy to be blessed with another child." Kenji exclaimed elatedly, although he was puzzled by her apparent displeasure.

"And I, my dear, I wish my departed wife was here to share the joy of unexpected blessing; she would've been a most happy grandmother." The senior Araki said waited for Mistresses response, but she was silent and her hands were folded tight resting on lap.

"When you are feeling better, the joy of motherhood will elate you." Senior Araki said, and his gentle voice soothed Mistresses anxiety.

After Father left, Kenji closed the shoji sliding door, sat in front of Shizuka and took her hands; a gesture Mistress had never saw him do before.

"Shizuka, I wish to reveal my inner thoughts I have never voiced." Kenji began, but paused for a moment to collect his thoughts. "When I saw you for the first time, your exquisite beauty captivated my body and soul, without mercy, and I was consumed by the desire to posses you as my own. However, you have grown more beautiful today as a mature woman." Kenji said paused again, in a world dominated by chauvinistic male, openly admitting one's love to spouse was considered unmanly; in fact, this was a first time Kenji has actually voiced his love to her, and she did not know how to respond, but before he could precede Mistress interrupted.

"Please, no need for your confession. Sir," Mistress Shizuka pleaded.

"Dear Shizuka, please hear me, for I may not speak of my thoughts to you again. I am aware that you had to disregard your lifelong wish to be a teacher, because of my marriage proposal, and I have forced you into the marriage to be my wife. Furthermore, I knew you were in love with a young man." Kenji said, remorsefully.

"Sir Please…" Mistress begged. Not wishing to hear about her long-ago love affair she has buried deep in her heart when her father accepted the Araki family's marriage proposal.

"Shizuka, allow me just this once; I'll never speak of this matter again. I am aware speaking of love openly is considered unmanly, a taboo among us men. But many times I wanted to tell you how much I loved you, and how beautiful you are, but my male chauvinistic ego wouldn't allow it." Kenji continued.

The Mistress had her hands, uncomfortably held captive in Kenji's, and anxiously waited for Kenji to stop his confession, but he kept on.

"Today the news of our miracle has encouraged me to speak my love to you, without considering myself as any less of a man. Our

love—ahh—my love helped to create another child, and I am a blessedly happy man, proud father of our four sons and the child soon to be born." Kenji hesitated momentary, and he wanted to hug her and tell her he loved her, but the words did not made it out of his mouth; instead Kenji said, *"I-I-I shall leave you for now."* And he left the chamber. For the first time since their marriage, Shizuka was aware of Kenji's love for her, but she could not joyfully respond to him; only an uncomfortable feeling, because she did not love him.

Every evening in an illuminating soft chamber light, I groomed mistress, and as always admired her beauty helped her with a soft pale pink silk night robe. However, tonight, I sensed Mistress Shizuka's demeanor was, unlike her usual spurious coquettish, blushing bride to please her husband; but tonight Mistress was sitting on the thick double layers of futon anxiously waiting for her husband.

Upon his arrival, Kenji, felt something restive about Mistress's demeanor, contrary to his expectation of erotic submissive endowment ready to receive him. And her night robe was tightly wrapped about her, hesitantly asked for a permission to speak. Kenji was taken aback by Mistress's unusual request promptly granted her wish out of his curiosity.

The Mistress Shizuka has chosen her words carefully as she began,

"Dear husband, since the day I became your wife I have obeyed your wish faithfully and submitted myself to you with the best of my abilities. We're now blessed with four grown sons, who are strong and your trusted business partners. I at this moment have a child growing within me, and I must protect my child by taking care of myself. I'm begging your pardon please to understand, at my advanced age I pray no harm would befall upon us." Mistress Shizuka spoke

calmly, expecting Kenji's displeasure, or simply leaves her sight. But Kenji was in disbelief, hearing Shizuka speak to him in such manner, so Shizuka continued while she still had her courage wish to be excused until then. *"You spoke of your love for me, and I am overwhelmed, but please refrain yourself from touching me until this child is born safely and my body is healed. Please, sir."* Penitently Mistress Shizuka placed her hands palm down on floor in front of her and bowed deeply.

Kenji was taken aback; for it was the first time Mistress had voiced her demands. Concealing his astonishment, he left her side without a word.

After Kenji left her chamber, Mistress sat motionless, listening to her own words still racing in her mind and her hard pulsating heartbeats were pounding with her thoughts of I have committed a sin, speaking against my husband. The Mistress Shizuka has resigned herself to an inevitable wrath of alienation; however, Kenji acted as if all was well, and throughout the Mistresses pregnancy he left her alone at night.

Transfixed in her thoughts, Mistress did not realize I came in the room to help tuck her in the futon.

"Yes, Taka, I'm fatigued," she murmured in a barely audible voice.

"You look lovely, ma'am!" I praised her, and detecting a scent of rare yellow orchid's that has secretes the perfume, no others flower has, and the perfume was made especially for Mistress. To obtain such a perfume, Kenji has sent his men to jungle of the South America and find the rare yellow orchid to obtain perfume, with a message of not to return until find the perfume.

It was a gift for Mistress Shizuka, who often sat alone deep in her thoughts, and Kenji knew the reason.

Recalling when I first came uninvited, to the Araki estate, I was fifteen and my younger sister Yumi was just nine, we were uneducated daughters of a poor farmer, but apparently Mistress. Shizuka has realized both of us have an intelligent mind other servants lacked. I knew we had keen sense of cognitions, never needs to be told twice how to do our work.

I could not help to think about the day, a very rich man came riding on a rickshaw to take Yumi and me, and if we were taken by him, I would be a sex slave stripped of dignity as a human being, using my body to work off the huge sum of money father has received from the owner of prostitution house. Ironically, village girls talked about the man at the communal water wall, she want discovered by him, and they have dreamed of living in a nice big house wear a pretty kimono, and making love to a man would be her only work.

"I don't have to work in the field anymore, and fetch a bucket of water many times a day I don't have to wear the same old kimono, so worn that I can't patch it anymore." They said, closed their eyes and the minds to a hidden hell within that nice big house, colored by an erroneous tainted rainbow.

Led by karma, Yumi and I have walked in uninvited to Araki estate kitchen, when Senior Araki was taking his usual morning stroll in the garden, and he heard a sound of commotion coming from the kitchen prompted him to investigate.

Entering, he saw Yumi and I were sitting on the dirt floor, my face was touching dirt floor, and both of us had bowing to the middle-aged head servant, acting as if he caught a thief, while few of other servants stood by to watch the going on.

"Please—please, sir," I was pleading for mercy.

"What's the meaning of this?" The senior Araki demanded. Surprised by the sudden appearance of their master, the head

servant, I presumed, bowed deeply as did the others. *"What's the meaning of this? —explain,"* again, senior Araki demanded.

I lifted my face and tried to speak, but the head servant pushed me down, causing my head to hit the ground hard. And Yumi was crying in fear.

"It's nothing I can't handle sir. This beggar's been coming here time and time again for a handout, so I was about to throw her out, sir." Head servant spoke with an air of authority.

"Stop this bullishness at once; I will speak to this girl myself." The senior Araki stated sternly, and he turned to me, but senior Araki did not considered me as a beggar. *"Raise your face child; explain yourself."* His voice was gentle; I looked up to the senior Araki, and the pillar of the village I had been told so much about. *"What has brought you here, child?"* The senior Araki asked and his gentle gesture has encouraged me and I told my tale of woe, hands tightly clenched on my lap.

"My name Taka, we poor have two big brothers, baby sister, her name Yumi, work hard every day. Get up dark, go home dark. Today rich man come talk to father, want to buy Yumi and me. She young, nine year old, not know man—I mean h-h-how to... Pretty soon rich man come, we go to his whorehouse. My sister Yumi—she my baby sister—men beat her, hurt her, not do he want. I'm big, no get hurt. Please, sir, save me and Yumi, please—I work hard for you, Yumi work hard too," I pleaded.

In an era I was born, it was a common practice among the poor to kill newborn female infants, the reason being, a dirt-poor family could not feed another mouth. However, a newborn male would be spared, because he will be put to work as soon as he could pick up a shovel or carry a basket, and if a male infant had a pretty face, he would be kept alive until he was six years old, when he could be sold as a boy-toy prostitute worth double or triple the price of a female.

Yumi and I have been allowed to live, however, my instinct warranted me the reason for us being alive, because Yumi and me was to be sold to a prostitution, and my father was waiting for a chance to get his hands on a windfall. My father wouldn't sell his own daughters? I have denied the suspicion, until I saw the rich man come to the house. I realized then my father's cynicism was proven true; he wanted to be a rich man himself, the truth shocked me to the core even though I have suspected all along. But seeing a pitiful sight of my father sitting on the ground, bowing to that man brought a lump in my throat.

"Say no more, Taka; I can see you are a hardworking, honest child. I will accept you and your sister Yumi as my servants, and you two will be given the instruction of your duties." Hearing his words, I felt my anxiety vanish, but it returned just as quickly.

"I thank you kindly, sir, but father angry, lose money not let us go," I told. My voice quivered with fear of my father.

"Not to worry, Taka. My man will be bearing my words for your father." And he signaled the servant to go.

I did not know it at the time, but the senior Araki has paid off our debt.

I sat on the ground, quietly chanted Zen, and thank Buddha for a good fortune bestowed on Yumi and me, and we have served Mistress Shizuka from that day on, as seeing pictures of a long ago memory flashes in my mind.

Yumi and I had predetermined mission to protect Mistress Shizuka's yet-to-be-born child, who was destined to become an orphan at a very young age. Moreover, the entire family would be crossing the path of fate, and their thread of life would be severed in the near future.

Yumi and I were given a duty to take care of Mistress Shizuka, and we learned our duties quickly. Every morning I placed steaming hot green tea on the bedside table for Mistress Shizuka, but this particular morning Mistress told us to remain for a moment, because she had an important matter to inform us.

"Listen carefully." Mistress has begun to explain about the importance of education. *"As you know, I am carrying a child, and Taka,—you will be the trusted caregiver of my infant; thus you and Yumi must learn to read, write, and speak proper sentences. I will teach both of you until you have learned your lessons."* While Mistress was talking to me, I began to weep; puzzled by my tears Mistress demanded an explanation. I gathered my best ability to speak and explained with my quivering voice.

"Ma'am, Yumi and me poor no school, every day I look neighbor chil'ren go school all pretty carry books. I cry see from field, I make Father angry." I paused to calm myself. *"Five year old I work, my brothers and father yell work harder, and I try but my shovel heavy, hard to pick up. Yumi born, Mother carries her on her back all day. Yumi and I go find clams pick good weeds make supper. Senior Araki saved us and you learn Yumi and me how to read and write. Thank you, ma'am, we good, learn everything,"* I promised sincerely.

Mistress Shizuka has requested permission from her father-in-law to educate Yumi and I, explaining the girls' intelligence was lying undeveloped, and they must be educated to be her infant's caregivers. However, her request was denied for a reason of *"No need to educate mere servants."* But the Mistress was adamant, and stressing the importance of educating us girls. Stating,

Only an educated mind would comprehend and know how to survive a possible predicament or emergency, which could arise at any given moment. They must be taught to use their intelligence, enable them to make educated decisions, as they will be my child's care providers and when an emergency would occur, it requires an immediate decision to save my child's life. Moreover, if the care giver is educated, my child will have a cushion of intelligent mind, whatever the situation is, not to be influenced by ignorance. Mistress has defined her wish.

The senior Araki was impressed by Mistresses foresight, thus the permission was granted with his blessing.

Every evening after our chores were done promptly we came for lessons, and to Mistress Shizuka's amazement, we have eagerly learned all we were taught, just as a bone-dry sponge soaks up every droplet of water, and we have excelled amazingly well in all of our studies; also the excellence of our academic aptitude was beyond the expectation of any schoolmaster. I became masterful in creative writing, especially the haiku, and received accolades in honor of my excellence.

Yumi, along with her skill for language, she had an extraordinary talent for the art of Japanese brush painting and silk screen embroidery, and she made a stunning kimono gown embroidered with exquisite chrysanthemums of gold, silver, red, and pink for the baby. Shizuka and all who viewed it were greatly impressed by the young Yumi's skill.

An early hour of February 22, 1932 Mistress Shizuka gave birth to a new life through a long hard labor, brought a female infant safely into the world.

"It's a girl child, ma'am!" The midwife said elatedly, as she peered into Mistresses sweat-drenched face. Trying to focus her eyes on the infant she had given birth to a moment ago.

"My baby, is she—? Is she—?" Mistress has tried to ask, but her tired voice conveyed she had just gone through the long and hard birth of a child, and Mistress could not complete her sentence.

"You have a beautiful girl baby, ma'am. The child is perfect, and she has a head full of fine black hair." I said and gently placed the infant already asleep, wrapped in a soft blanket in Mistress

Shizuka's arms, I sat and watched her looking lovingly at her first-born daughter, she has never expected to have at her an age, and named her daughter Tami.

Miss Tami was born into an old wealthy family, visualizing child's future will be happy and secure; and seeing an image of her daughter growing up. However, Mistress Shizuka has not suspected another war would assail their lives, to the point of holocaustic pandemonium, annihilating the hopes and futures of every living being, including the Araki family.

Seventh day of the child's birth, Shinto sacrament requires the newborn infant to be anointed by the Shinto god. Customarily the grandmother carries the infant adorned in a white silk ceremonial kimono, and she led the family to the Shinto temple. However, I was appointed as an infant carrier, and the Mistress Shizuka and her husband Kenji followed behind me.

The day of sacrament, servants were scrubbing and cleaning the premises from top to bottom, and gardeners were manicuring the garden with the utmost care, while the special menu of foods being prepared to celebrate the occasion. Grandfather led the Shinto priest throughout the estate carrying a bowl of burning incense while priest performed exorcises, leaving a trail of blue smoke.

After the exorcism ritual was done, Grandfather sequestered himself in the family shrine, meditated for Tami's happy future, visualizing a stunningly beautiful grown-up Tami; but never did he suspect his precious granddaughter would thrust into a tragic demise.

Mistress Shizuka has focused only upon nurturing her daughter, whom by a miracle, came late in her life, and she no longer attended any social function with Kenji even though duty called.

In the summer month's traditional holidays to be celebrated, and the seventh day of the seventh month was the annual Festival of

Stars, and the Araki family prepared for the festivity with the added joy of a pretty-as-a-flower little girl and she watched the servants erecting the traditional tall bamboo in an entrance of the estate.

Slender bamboo branches had the many colorful strips of paper tied to them, all dancing in the breeze as if dodging unpredictable fingers of wind trying to tickle them. Miss Tami was mesmerized by many pretty strips dancing in a breeze, began to dance merrily around bamboo. The Star Festival to be celebrated for the love of Vega and the Weaver.

The legend foretold they were in love against the law of universe, promised to each other they would be together for an eternity. The penalty was decreed upon, Vega and the Weaver, and they must part for an entire year. But the leniency was permitted; enabled lovers to be united for a brief moment, on the seventh day of the seventh month. So to cherish their precious moment of joy, the beholders who wish upon the stars had written love poems, on the strips of colorful rainbow tablets, tied to the branches of a tall bamboo to be displayed in front of the house.

In the following month of August, Bon an important Buddhist holiday was celebrated, and on this day the spirits of ancestors will return home for three days to be with their loved ones. So to welcome them, every household was cleanse and purify to welcome visiting ancestors'. Pink water lily blossoms were pedestals, for spirits of the ancestors', surround by the season's flowers for the traditional homecoming festivity.

An abundance of foods will be prepared for this occasion, to be shared with relatives and the visiting neighbors who come to pay their respects; they lights incense and offer a prayer for the ancestral spirits. A priest will visit homes to perform a special prayer ritual for the occasion, receiving a gratuity and a tray of food as a token of appreciation.

During the three days, families will make traditional homage to the shrine, bearing a monetary offering for the Buddha, asking him to ensure their ancestral spirits' safe arrival home. Then on the evening of the third day, the spirits will depart on board of a small boat built for their return journey, loaded with specially prepared foods and the season's flowers for their grand parting. The ceremonial boat will be decorated with many white paper lanterns strung by a rope from the mast to bow and stern.

In the milky descending dusk, the Araki family followed the boat carried by their servants in white ceremonial attire. *"Watt shoi, watt shoi,"* they shouted in unison, to keep in pace as proceeded to the seashore.

The candles in the lanterns were lit and the boat was launched onto the ebbing tides, while the entire Araki family watched the boat sailed to a faraway sprits' world, until it disappeared beyond the waves. I carried Miss Tami, and Araki family made homage to the Buddhist shrine, Yumi walked with me, to pray for the departed souls', and in an appreciations monetary offering was placed in a tray on a table, in front of the statute, and the family knelt in front of a huge gold statue of Buddha, lowered heads in prayer.

When we were returning to the carriage, for a fleeting moment Mistress Shizuka saw a man she had not forgotten in three decades; although his appearance has changed, but the man was unmistakably Takeshi, her never forgotten love from long ago. Mistress Shizuka's heart skipped a beat and leaped up to her throat, an emotional jolt threw her off balance and caused her to stumble, an uncontrollable cry escaped her lips. Luckily her husband Kenji caught hold of her.

"Begging your pardon sir, I'm very clumsy these days." Mistress Shizuka apologized, unable to control her quivering voice.

Unfortunately, the minor incident has caught the Takeshi's

attention, and for a moment their eyes met. At that instant they knew their love for each other was still in flame after so many years. Takeshi stood there unable to look away, following the carriage carrying Mistress. Shizuka until it was out of his sight. Puzzled by his wife's demeanor Kenji stared at her ashen face, surmising she must have seen someone or something.

Desperately trying to regain her composure, Mistress Shizuka closed her eyes, attempting to hide wallowing up tears but spilled down her cheeks. Shizuka chanted Zen in silence, and a moment carriage stopped, without waiting for my assist, she has quickly disembarked carriage, entered her chamber to avoid inquisitive eyes.

The heat of the summer days became intolerable, so every morning I carried buckets of water from the kitchen to fill a tub out on the verandah, for the mistress to cool herself by bathing in the sun warmed water.

Every year during the dog days of summer, the Araki family has retreated to their summer home on Mount Unzen, a volcanic mountain a mile above sea level, and graced with an eternal spring. Masses of thriving Azaleas have covered an entire mountaintop, and its blossoms of many color blooming profusely year round. Miss Tami and I took a walk to see so many blossoms while submersed in its perfume. Mount Unzen was born of volcano, stood atop a volcanic fault, but lies in dormant for the past two hundred years, but an imminent danger of erupting was not present.

In 1932, the year Miss Tami was born, for the first time in history, Japan was not engaged in a war; peace prevailed and the entire country has gained the opportunities of economic prosperity, as the citizens across the country has enjoyed their peaceful existence.

Araki real estate business has rolled along with a tide of growing economy, prospering to a giant enterprise, but lately grandfather's health had begun to decline, so Kenji thought it was in his father's best interest to retire and enjoy the fruits of his hard earned success. Considering the delicate nature of the situation, Kenji has prepared a speech carefully in his mind before he approached his father, but to his surprise Father agreed without an objection.

The senior Araki knew in his heart, his productive days were over and more often than not, he began to experience fatigue brought on by a lack of stamina unable to keep up with the daily business demands, so to be free of the responsibilities were welcome relief.

Since the retirement, the senior Araki had ample free time at hand; he spent much of his time with his granddaughter every day, often sitting next to the sleeping infant, in her nursery unable to take his eyes off her. *"An apple of my eye."* He murmured with a smile his aged face, and as always he saw a vision of his wife's smiling face, while waiting patiently for Granddaughter Tami to wake, and then *"She's awake!"* He called out in a whisper.

I wrapped the baby in a blanket and laid her down in a carriage, watched the senior Araki, once feared as a shrewd business mogul, cooing to the love of his life pushing the carriage slowly around the courtyard, enjoying pleasure of his cherished time with Grandchild.

The third day of March was a symbolic Peach Blossom holiday for all the young girl children, and her family celebrated with a traditional display of miniature dolls of the royal family on a tiered showcase.

Seated on the top tier were the royal Prince and Princess, each attired in the traditional gold and red layers of the ceremonial robes. On the second tier were their servants and the royal carriage pulled by oxen; the third tier held warriors attired in their splendid shiny battle armor; fourth were holiday offerings of foods; and on the fifth tier was a large diamond-shaped three-tiered rice cake pink, green, and white were placed on the elongated rose-colored lacquer table. Branches of pink peach blossoms were gracefully arranged on each side, beautifully complementing the entire setting.

Because Miss Tami was born near the end of February, there had not been enough time to prepare for her first Peach Blossom Festival, so two pink flowering peach trees were planted that year in her honor. But for the next year's festival, specific orders were already sent to the famous doll makers in Kyoto, and plans were in the works to build Tami's teahouse furnished with custom made child size furniture.

In an addition, pair of peacocks was sent from the East Indies to complement Miss Tami's fairy tale teahouse, surrounded by a miniature garden. When the teahouse was partially completed, the Shinto priest was summoned to perform the exorcism and blessing of the house. An open invitation to the ceremony was posted at the Shinto shrine, informing the public that they were invited to the customary tossing of rice cakes thrown from the rafters. The villagers talked excitedly about the upcoming event, which was the topic of the year; and for the first time the Araki estate's gates would be opened to the public, and everyone would be permitted to enter the premises.

A slow uphill carriage driveway led up to the five acres of meticulously groomed ground, and three-tiered Pagoda shrine was in a center of garden. All visitors were instantly turned to the magnificent shrine standing on an island in the center of the garden, which was encircled by a dry river lined with white pebbles. An enchanting red-and-gold arched bridge straddled over the river. There was a scent of jasmine in air and the grand view of the valley below as far as to the distant horizon.

The magnificent three-story family shrine of red, gold, and black, with elegant blue pagoda roofs, shone under the blue sky. Peering down from under the eaves was an enormous intricately carved mythical golden dragon with intimidating large black eyes, its long body of gold scales wrapped around the upper walls beneath the eaves.

Cherry trees lined the estate perimeter, and the heavenly scent of sweet olive jasmine permeated the air from clusters of tiny white flowers. An earth tone and white marbled flagstone walkway snaked throughout the entire garden, where the dwarf pine trees, weeping willows, and giant pink and gray quartz granites were placed majestically to complement the garden. At the far end of the estate, blossoming red camellia hedges discreetly concealed the servants' quarters.

The villagers gazed around with gaping mouths, astonished and speechless, marveling at the extraordinary beauty of the Araki estate.

In accordance with the custom, rice cakes were to be thrown from atop the newly elected rafter, but Grandfather feared that would create mass chaos and may cause an injury to someone, so the rice cakes would be wrapped in napkin, which embossed with Araki coat of arms, villagers has never seen it before, and handed out.

An early morning hour, people were already beginning to gather, forming a line at the entrance gate. They came from as far as the city of Hakata, twelve-plus kilometers, four plus miles away, not only for the ceremony, but to see the interior of the famously rich Araki estate.

The carriage arrived with a priest on board, and more carriages followed carrying invited dignitaries for the celebration party. As the carriages passed through the gates, a few people ran through the open gates and gained entry to the estate, but the servants ushered them back out until the permitted time. The event was a grand success, and the conversations among awestruck villagers continued. They talked about the Araki's spare no expense festivity, of the very wealthy and their luxuriant lifestyle they could only dream about.

By midsummer, Miss Tami's teahouse was completed, and the strolling pair of peacocks intensified the heavenly atmosphere of the garden of Shangri-La.

Following year's peach blossom celebration, Mistress Shizuka dressed Miss Tami in the embroidered colorful silk kimono; Yumi has made especially for Miss Tami's third birthday, and visited the Buddha's shrine to pray for Miss Tami's safe passage through her third year's devil's curse.

The Buddha's proverb forewarned that a girl child at an age of three, seven, and a boy child at an age of five are vulnerable to the devil's postulate, so to protect the child, parent's offers monetary gift and ask Buddha for his protection, to ward off the devil's evil curse until the child is a year older.

In spite of her cursed age of three, Miss Tami did not have even a sniffle; and she began to talk with her own tongue. Grandfather's heart would melt, when Miss Tami looked up with her large dark eyes and said, "Grandpapa."

"My precious princess." He whispered and hugged her gently.

"Walk, Grandpapa?" Miss Tami would say putting her tiny hand in his, and they walked leisurely around the garden. Oftentimes Mistress Shizuka would join them, and they stopped to watch the peacocks spread open their magnificent tail feathers

of iridescent blue, jade, and gold. Seeing the colorful magic, Miss Tami let out a squeal with delight; Grandfather smiled with pleasure, and he thought to himself it was all worth the while.

Stopping to rest at Miss Tami's tea house after walk in the garden, Yumi would be waiting to serve sweet cakes and hot tea for Grandfather and Shizuka, and a cup of milk for Miss Tami and enjoy the tranquil moment. I brought a wheelchair for Grandfather, and sit Miss Tami on his lap, I wheeled them back to the residents' quarters.

At an age of three, Miss Tami began to show an extraordinary intelligence and photographic memory. One day Mistress Shizuka heard Miss Tami's voice and sounds as if she was reading a story. Walking up to her child, Mistress Shizuka was astounded to find, three years old daughter was sitting on the floor with an opened fairy tale book resting on her out stretched legs, and her mother read to her night before. Incredibly, Miss Tami has memorized the story, a word for word beginning to an end.

Hearing the Miss Tami's extraordinary aptitude, Grandfather was greatly impressed, and he suggested teaching his granddaughter a second language of English, so the youngest son, Shingo, a graduate of UCLA, was appointed as her tutor and every day after Miss Tami awoke from her nap, Shingo and his baby sister would spend the afternoon conversing in English.

Chapter 4: Chaos

In 1944, foreboding ill karma veiled over the Japan, but General Tojo has ignored the ominous shroud and continued to beat the war drum, in spite of government's bankrupted war chest, unable to support the demanding war expenses; inevitably, worthless paper money was printed and flooded the market, skyrocketing inflation plagued country's economy, and bottomless black market flourished, people were surviving a day to day by grasping straws.

There were no more blaring victory songs, no more propaganda hype, and the banners bearing war slogans were torn and hung by nails; some of them was weather beaten and tattered fallen on the ground, but no one cared because people were robbed of their will to live. Upholding the law was a thing of the past; only the strong and cunning ruled.

Refugees had to live wherever space was available, in makeshift huts, and they walked long distances to the farming villages hoping to buy some food, but the farmer would not accept the newly printed worthless paper money for their goods. Refugees were afraid, seeing a shotgun farmer had protecting his crops from looters.

In desperation, they have consumed weeds, birds, rodents, reptiles, frogs, insects, and even pet dogs or cats if any could be found. As a result, the frail and aged did not have a chance for survival.

Lately, a buzzing rumor was spreading among the people about the threat of an air raid, and their gut instinct forewarned it was imminent. And just as their senses has predicted, the bombing began targeting populated cities and industrial areas. Crowded houses built of wood and paper went up in flames as if dried up old newspaper, people ran from their burning homes with only the clothes they wore.

Having nowhere to go or to hide, refugees searched for any structure still left standing, hoping it would render some protection from the elements of weather, but those remaining structure, if any was already occupied. Consequently, without a choice, people stayed where their house once stood, and using the debris for firewood, that was once the wall and posts of their house, and ate whatever were available, even to steal from unsuspecting fellow refugees.

The affluent Araki family lived in a sparsely populated farming village in the Kumamoto prefecture, on the northern Kyushu Island miles away from the heavily industrialized city of Fukuoka, which encompassed steel mills, oil refineries, coal mines, and an international seaport.

Grandfather Araki had a bomb shelter built underneath the family shrine on their estate, to protect his family from air attacks. Although being the small village, he was assumed to be safe from the bombing, but there were school buildings resembling a factory from air.

One day the front page of the newspaper read, enemy submarines in the Japan Sea! That meant submarines had infiltrated the guarded Korean Strait, and the fleets of aircraft carriers were not far behind; in fact, the enemy invasion of the Japanese homeland was only a matter of time. Rumors were running rampantly, born of vulnerable minds: *"We'll be all killed."* frightened folks said to one another, visualizing their homesteads destroyed, and the men were abducted as slaves and the women as sex slaves, so they dug tunnels to hide.

Lately, strangers were coming to the Araki estate every night, and they stayed behind the closed door for hours on end with grandfather and Kenji. Miss Tami, thirteen years old the youngest of the Araki, was the most frightened by the intruding nightly visits of those strangers, but one-day grandfather has revealed the reason for their visits to relieve his worried family.

Explaining, *"Those strangers were the government agents. They came with demands in the name of the Emperor to take the Araki assets, money, stocks, bonds, real estate holdings, and anything of value to be donated to finance the war; they even demanded the deed to the Araki estate."* However, grandfather had staunchly refused to give up the estate, knowing full well he could be imprisoned as a traitor for his unpatriotic behavior to the Emperor.

Not only the wealthy, but also the poor were targeted to give up more of their positions, and anything that could be forged into weapons. Moreover, it was mandatory to remove gold or silver caps from their teeth, and wedding rings to be donated in the name of the Emperor. Thus for the first time in the Araki family legacy, the family was reduced to the rank of paupers; having all of their fortunes extorted until none was left. Grandfather had to dismiss all his servants, with his apology, because he was unable to keep them employed. However, to his surprise, the servants expressed their wish to stay on to serve the family in time of need; they would not leave their master who stood by to aid them when they were in need of help.

"Want not until the victory!" The newly created government propaganda slogans were posted everywhere, but to the tired and disheartened citizens who have lost their loved ones and what was left of their livelihood the new slogan was a kick in their gut.

One day Mistress Shizuka summoned Yumi and me to her chamber, because she had an urgent matter that could not delay another moment, to protect her gems she hid from the Government Agents.

"Both of you listen carefully; I have a very serious matter to confide in you." Mistress began. We looked intensely at her, not knowing what to expect, and Mistress has gestured for us to come closer and then lowered her voice to a whisper. *"Perhaps you realize our future may be doomed. As for Grandfather, my husband and me, we do not matter because our lives are nearly spent. But Tami is still very young, and she has not had a chance to live her life. And there is nothing of value left in our possession to provide for her future; however, I have secretly withheld my collection of gems."*

Mistress listened for any sound of footsteps, but only a whispering breeze flowing through the bamboo leaves. The gems were a collection of precious stones amounting to an inestimable value, which Mistress Shizuka had secretly hidden from the government agents, for Tami's secure future and live her life with dignity.

"I've made a conscious decision not to consult my husband or the father-in-law about the gems, but I am certain they knew about it and kept quiet."

Yumi and I were in a total awe, watched Mistress Shizuka went over to her vanity table and brought out a beautiful shiny black lacquer box from the drawer. Our eyes were widened to see a lacquer box adorned with inlaid gold trees with jade leaves, mother-of-pearl cranes with garnet crowns, standing in a silver pond with delicate pink water lily blossoms, which created a lifelike scene; even the tree bark was sculpted of gold.

"Ohhh, Mistress, this is a beautiful box!" I have exclaimed, and Yumi nodded her head rapidly, and we were unable to speak or take our eyes off the box of exquisite beauty, both of us have never seen it before.

Mistress Shizuka removed the top of the three-tiered box, revealing many exquisite and rare natural pearls of rings, necklaces, brooches, and hair ornaments. The second tier had sapphires, rubies, amethysts, opals, jade, garnets, and countless pieces of precious stones creating sparkling dancing prisms. The third tier was the deepest of all, containing many diamonds of characteristic cut and sizes set in gold brooches, platinum rings, necklaces, and many more loose pieces, all of them have glistened with a brilliant clear hue and the slightest of movement has cast hypnotizing spell.

"Girls, pay attention to what I am about to tell you, but first I must have your pledge of secrecy, because you two will be the carriers of these gems. However, I do strongly emphasize the consequence of the gems being discovered; conceal them with caution.

"My sixth sense warns me that an imminent fate is near; I fear we'll be crucified, though I've tried to dismiss such a thought out of my mind." Mistress Shizuka paused for a moment; and we were dumbfounded as Mistress Shizuka continued.

"You two were the only people I can trust with my daughter, with confidence. I am placing Tami in your care after I'm gone and as for my sons, they are not coming back, I feel it in my soul.

"These gems will provide the necessities for all of you to live

comfortably, but also be very discreet in dispensing them, and furthermore, destroy the jewelry box to ensure no one sees it. Have I made myself clear?" Mistress Shizuka has ended her talk and looking at us for a sign of confirmation.

"Yes, ma'am, we'll guard Miss Tami with our lives," I answered.

"As you know, the senior Araki has rescued us from becoming sex slaves, and we made our pledge that someday a chance would come to repay the kindness senior Araki had given us. Furthermore, you gave us an education to be proud of.

"Our gratitude is beyond the words can express. But please, begging your pardon, ma'am, we cannot bring ourselves to destroy this beautiful box," I pleaded.

"I appreciate your sentiment, but consider for a moment. If someone sees you with this jewelry box, the word will get around faster than you think, and eventually will reach the government agent's ear. You can then assume the jewels will be confiscated, and we will all be prosecuted." Mistress Shizuka emphasized.

"My thousand pardons, ma'am." I apologized, realizing the grave consequences should the box be discovered, but knowing I could never be able to destroy such a beautiful box. Shizuka waved off the apology and asked for another favor.

"I have a small decanter of perfume, which was a gift from my husband."

"Yes, I know the perfume, ma'am."

"Give it to Tami, when the time comes, because it meant a great deal for my husband to go as far as he did to obtain the perfume from a rare orchid growing in a South American jungle."

"Ma'am, but how will I know when the right time arrives?" I asked, being puzzled.

"You'll know." Was all she said?

Later that night, I made two amulets with a piece of an old fabric, and threaded a long enough string in an opening to put around our nick, and by pulling open and close tight. And equally divided the gems in halves put the gems into it, and we wore amulet around neck under our garment.

At the beginning of the war, preparations were in the works to implement Antiaircraft Artillery to be installed at the strategic points, but General Tojo was against the idea, and adamantly disagreed boasting, "Should an attempt be made by the enemies, the Shinto god will create a fury of wind to blow them away." Ironically, even if the artillery were installed it would have been rendered useless, because not a shell was left for its use. Having no defenses, the air raids continued without being counter attacked.

Air raids became more frequent, as the B-29s flew over Kyushu Island en route to and from their targeted areas, triggering a warning siren to go off. Ironically the people gotten used to the repetitious sound of siren and began to ignore it, and then one morning siren sounded right on time as usual, and the people has automatically assumed the B-29s were heading north, high up in the sky.

But on this particular morning, the warning siren, which repeated in long intervals has instantly change to a rapid short-interval, a sound of being under an actual attack, and then in a mere moment, loud heavy sounds of approaching planes drowned out the blaring siren, as instantly the Grumman fighter planes were overhead in low altitude as if bees flying out from a broken hive, began dive-bombing, dropping the incendiary napalm bombs over the village point blank.

The ground shook as the bombs were exploding everywhere, just as the epicenter of a violent earthquake, and an inferno engulfed the village. Terrified people ran for their lives, scurrying into the crudely dug shelters, only to realize they were trapped under the raging inferno and cooked alive.

As night fell, the bombing ceased and the planes were gone, but the blazing bloody red flames lit up the night sky, and few shadowy figures Silhouetted visible against the backdrop of the still violently raging fire.

The Araki family ran to their bomb shelter when the air attack began, and Mistress Shizuka held the petrified Miss Tami in a bear hug, and Yumi and I shook uncontrollably with fear. The bomb shelter was equipped with fresh air vents for comfort, but ironically those comfort features had turned against them, sending in the intolerable heat and suffocating black smoke, and billowing flames howled as though a demon from hell was consuming the estate, and pushed horrorstruck Tami into an uncontrollable scream, and then she fell quiet. Tami fainted. "Get out!" I screamed, but only a hiss came through my burnt throat. I got down on my hands and knees, groping to find the way out from the bomb shelter. Then I felt Miss Tami's long tresses I grabbed hold of her and dragged the unconscious girl out.

Regaining some strength from breathing less tainted air, I returned for Yumi and the rest of the family, nearly succumbing to the thick smoke, and I have managed to drag out the unconscious Yumi, and then immediately doubled back for Mistress Shizuka but to my dismay, Mistress Shizuka, Kenji, and the senior Araki were lifeless, suffocated by smoke. Gasping for air I scurried out from the bomb shelter, sobbing uncontrollably, having failed to save the three people I loved and worshipped. I lay on the ground beside Miss Tami and Yumi, drained of all my strength.

Daybreak has revealed the horror of pandemonium: In an overnight the beautiful estate and lovely garden were reduced to a heap of smoldering debris. Hopelessness and disbelief took all my incentives for a reason to live, but I had to find the means to doctor Miss Tami and Yumi's blistering wounds. Our eyes were swollen, and tears spilled from Tami and Yumi between their closed eyelids and rolled down their raw cheeks.

I put aside my own pain, from burn and discomfort, to find shelter and food, most of all water. But first, I must take care of the deceased mustering every bit of my strength and dragged out the three corpses, covered in black soot. I have managed to pull them one by one atop of a still smoldering pile of debris and fanned the embers until the funeral pyre was lit. Tami, Yumi, and I have knelt in respect, offered the Buddha's sacred prayer, as witnessing the bodies of three people slowly engulfed by the pyre, sending the three souls to heaven. We sat and prayed until the bodies were cremated.

I was faced with the urgent need to prepare the shelter, realizing the only solution was the bomb shelter, but needs to cover the earthen floor, and the care for Tami and Yumi's wounds could not be put off any longer moreover, dire need of food and water were urgent. I had Mistress Shizuka's precious gems concealed under the cloths I wore, but the gems were of no help there was no one to trade with.

I went in search of anything edible, hoping may be some food still remaining in the kitchen area, probing among the debris, pulling out anything I got my hands on, but all I found was more unrecognizable charred debris. Luckily, in the residence area, I spotted a part of Grandfather's wheelchair protruding from among the debris, I dug it out and brushed the dirt off, and to my amazement, and the chair was still workable. There were pieces of burnt clothing and futons, I pounded the dust off, quickly piled my findings on the wheelchair returned to bomb shelter. Although we had to contend with a pungent burnt odor, but being thankful not have to lie on the bare ground.

In a blink of an eye the world we knew was gone, and my mind could not comprehend the horror of the drastic sudden change; my ability to discern between real and fantasy spiraled out of control, as my mind floated in and out of my brain.

I dreamt of bombs falling and the fire burning. I can't breathe! Everybody get out! I need to go after yesterday's sunup when all was well, but it is moving away faster and faster. *"Wait! Wait for me!"* I shouted unable to catch up to yesterday's dawn; and I was pulled down into a bottomless nightmare. And the shocked by horror of pandemonium has drove me to be disorientated, sealed me in an erroneous word.

Since the fire, Miss Tami has not spoken a word; unable to grasp the horror of sudden change and in denial, retreated into an erroneous womb to shield her in. We did not have any food or water for nearly three days, and I no longer felt any hunger pains.

"I must find food, anything that could be eatable?" I urged myself, trying to crawl out from the bomb shelter, but overcame by an excruciating fatigue I never made it out, fall right into a vivid dreams of the bombs exploding, fire, smoke, and the death of my beloved masters again and again.

Awakened at dawn, I informed Yumi and the Miss Tami of my intention of finding food, made my way into the village, desperately fighting the faint from hunger, praying my unsteady legs would not give out on me. As I came upon where the village had been until three days ago, I walked into a pungent odor of ratting flesh and haze of smoke smoldering from heaps of blackened debris, stung my eyes and tears to wall up.

My knees buckled, and I craw on my hands and knees, as lashed out at myself to *"Get up. Get up!"*

Just then my hands felt cool grass; and then I saw a weathered old farmhouse standing beyond overgrown bushes. *"Oh, the honorable Buddha—that's my house. How did I get here?"* I said in disbelief, forcing myself to stand up and approached closer to barely standing an old house.

Holding onto the doorway I peered into a dark interior, *"Mama,"* I called, but not a sound came from inside, and I called out *"Father"* and then my brothers by their names, but no answer came. I walked into a silent interior lit only by streaks of sunlight shining through the holes in the roof, revealing an open cooking pit still intact in the hard packed earthen floor of kitchen, a had ash covered unburned wood. Family burned the fire in the cooking pit to keep warm in the cold night.

Opposite of the cooking pit was a wood platform on stilts, where we ate meals and stained dark from many years of living, there were some utensils left lying about. I recognized the chipped rice bowls, and few odds and ends, seeing those familiar items, I felt nostalgic. However, after gaining enough mental strength, I walked out to the family's small farming field across the way, recalling once I toiled alongside of my brothers and father from dawn to dusk many years ago, but the field was covered with nothing but sprawling overgrown weeds.

Standing on an edge of the field, for the first time since Yumi and I left home, I had a sense of being at home; an ironic moment of comfort flashed in my mind.

I was looking at a field I have work so hard, and then I spot a familiar sweet potato vines among the weeds, grabbed the vine and traced it down to the ground dug away the dirt with my hands, until exposed a sweet potato; it was a sight to behold. Quickly I dug up a sweet potato, brushed off the dirt, took a bite, and another bite and then another, filling my mouth with crunchy sweet morsels. The family must have left in haste, leaving the crops unharvested, and I ate more sitting on the weedy ground savoring the taste of a sweet potato.

And then an idea struck: We should relocate here to the farmhouse, and I could care for Miss Tami and Yumi. Moreover, if my memory serves right, there was a geothermal hot spring we used to bathe, and an abundance of aloe plants growing in the nearby field, which were crucially important medicinal healing elements to cure burns and cuts, also the thermal mineral water contained sulfur which has an element of antibiotic.

The farmers were subjected to wounds that had often results in an infection, and to cure it, they used abundantly available sulfur and aloe. I thanked Buddha for leading me to the solution I have sought so desperately, and then dug more sweet potatoes hurried back to the estate.

I returned to the bomb shelter and buried sweet potatoes in the hot ashes to roast, when become soft tasted like honey morsels, we even consumed the skins, savoring every bite and sipping hot water.

For the first time since the bombing; we were able to relax, sipping hot water using a metal teakettle I found at the farmhouse, even Miss Tami seemed to come out from her mental lock, but still she was unable to ask about her parents and grandfather.

In the evening, when a daylight still remaining, I brought up my an imperative plans to relocate, telling Miss Tami and Yumi the move was in our best interest, explaining about the hot spring and the farmhouse, we decided to make the move next day.

Early the following morning, I inspected the ground all around to salvage anything that could be of use, but finding nothing I carried Miss Tami out from the bomb shelter on my back and piled all our belongings onto the wheelchair, and she sat on a top of it.

For the first time Miss Tami was faced with the ruins of her family's estate, had a good look at the devastation, realizing debris that was all left of the beautiful estate, she began to sob.

"Where's my parents and grandfather?" Miss Tami asked, not remembered about the funeral pyre, since nature expurgated horrid memory to protect the impressionable adolescent's mind.

I did not have a word to comfort Miss Tami, who was orphaned at the tender age of thirteen. I hugged the sobbing child.

"Miss Tami, I beg your forgiveness for not telling you sooner, but with my heavy heart, I must inform that your family has perished in the fire, and we too have barely escaped with our lives. I dragged you and Yumi from the bomb shelter, and then rushed back for your family, nearly succumbing to the smoke and heat, but it was too late.

"The following day, I cremated the bodies and buried them where your lovely teahouse garden was."

Chapter 5: Refugees

As we neared the village foul odor invaded our senses, and stench became stronger as we advanced further, it was a smell coming from decomposed bodies of old and sick. When the bombing begun, people have fled the inferno left their old and sick behind, unable to carry them. Tragically those unfortunate people have expired where they sat.

Quickening strides and holding our breath to avoid the strong rotting stench, we ran maneuvering around many potholes and debris on the path, trying not to upset the wheelchair, while Miss Tami was holding onto the arms of wheelchair, and Yumi followed behind desperately hold down her first meal, turned into a path lead to the farmhouse, gasping for air unable to run anymore.

After breathing has calmed, I noticed the surrounding field; the trees had green leaves standing amidst grasses and blooming wildflowers. Amazing to see such a beauty of nature, versus heaps of debris and blackened bare trees.

"Taka, where are we?" Miss Tami asked, mesmerized by the surrounding greenery.

"Miss Tami, this path will take us to the farmhouse; it's only a short distance from here," I said to assure her.

Shortly we came upon a small weather-beaten, barely standing farmhouse, and Yumi stared at familiar-looking old house with gaping holes and cracks on walls. And then Yumi recalled it was long ago when her sister Taka took her away from this house. The sight of the familiar farmhouse triggered her faded, barely existing memory.

Yumi was only nine years old when she left hastily with her big sister Taka, and she did not give explanation of why they had to leave in such hurry; but seeing the look of fright on her big sister's face, Yumi felt a chilling fear that something terrible would happen if they stayed. But the reason was still unknown to her even to the present day.

Yumi began to sob, as the long ago memory of their sudden departure had spurred an emotional upheaval. I hugged my little sister to assure her all will be well.

"Taka, is this…? This house we are to live in this house?" Miss Tami asked, appalled by its appearance.

"Yes, Miss Tami, we're going to live here. Yumi and I will do our best to make your stay comfortable." I assured her, although I had no idea how to make this house livable. Wasting no time, Yumi and I began to inspect the interior, and the damage was just as severe as on the exterior, if it rained there would not be a dry spot in the house. We worked tirelessly to clear a spot for Miss Tami in front of the kitchen area, away from under the holes in the roof, where the family used to dine. We found tattered clothing, odds and ends of household items, but none of those gave any clue as to where the family might have gone. I surmised they must have fled the premises when the bombing began.

As a small child, I over heard about the conversations among the grownups, and they were talking about our distant cousins living in the foothills of Mount Unzen. The Mount Unzen stood in the center of the Shimabara Peninsula, which is a tropical village two hundred kilometers, 27 miles west across the Ariake Bay from where her family lived. Sparsely populated Shimabara was famous for producing bountiful crops from the fertile volcanic soil, and prized fishes were caught from the bay.

They must've gone there, where the food are plentiful, I have surmised.

Putting my thoughts aside, I left Miss Tami in care of Yumi and went out into the field for more sweet potatoes and wild berries, while I had my eyes appealed for the hot spring in vicinity, and remembering how my mother used to tend the wounds gathering the sulfur from hot spring, and using the remedy she concocted from gained knowledge, through years of experience. When need arises mother sent me to gather sulfur and aloes. Mother, please! I need your wisdom, I asked visualizing her image. And then from over yonder a wisp of steam arose, and I detected the unmistakable whiff of sulfur.

I run in a direction of raising steam, lured by the more pungent odor of sulfur, and I came upon the hot spring pool just as I remembered it.

There were massive deposits of yellow sulfur on the rocks and sand around the pond's edge, and aloe plants growing on each side of the stream, covering the entire hillside. *"Oh, my gracious Buddha, you have led me here to the pond. My gratitude for ever."* I thanked Buddha out loud and hurried home to relay my finding.

Hearing about hot spring pond, Miss Tami and Yumi wished to bathe immediately, since we have not bathe for some time. Gathering the pottery and old chopsticks wrapping them all in rags, Yumi and I have assisted Tami onto the wheelchair and pushed her out of the house. However, the task of maneuvering the wheelchair through the field was exceedingly difficult; the wheels sank into the soft ground. *"Begging your pardon, Miss Tami, but I must ask you to walk, as you can see the ground is too soft for the wheelchair."*

I apologized and wrapped Miss Tami's foot with rags and carefully helped her to stand, but her feet were still raw she grimace and grit her teeth in pain. *"Are you able to walk, Miss Tami?"* I asked, alarmed by Miss Tami's stiffness.

"Yes, let us go." Miss Tami has commanded and slowly we have proceeded forward, but after few yards the rags wrapped on her feet were soaked with blood. Alarmed by the sight of blood, immediately I picked Miss Tami up.

"Please forgive me Miss Tami; I know you're hurting." I apologized.

"No need for an apology, Taka, I'm fine." Miss Tami said, and then out of the blue…

"Taka, we have no money?" She questioned, caught me off guard, and it took me a moment to think of an answer; I realized the thought must have been on Miss Tami's mind for some time, and she started a conversation at this particular moment to draw her mind away from the pains in her feet. I have assured Miss Tami that all was well, no need to trouble herself with domestic matter, and then I changed the subject to explain about the hot spring pond that will heal her wounds.

After searching for a good place to set up a camp, I chose a spot further downstream where the flowing hot geothermal mineral water was comfortably cooled for bathing. Yumi spread rags in the shallow sandy riverbed for Miss Tami to lie where warm water soothes her body. Soon the hardened crusty body fluid melted away, releasing the garments that had been stuck to her wounds.

Carefully I rinsed Miss Tami's long matted hair; and while doing so, I had a good look at her swollen face for the first time; she was skin-and-bone. Tears walled up in my eyes and dropped into the water unnoticed. Yumi washed the soiled clothing and spread it over on the aloe plants to dry. All was well this peaceful afternoon.

"Are you all right, ma'am?" I asked, concerned by Miss Tami's silence.

"Yes Taka. Warm water feels very soothing; it's been a while since I bathed." Miss Tami said, and then she wished to be left alone.

"Miss Tami, I'm going down to the seashore not far from here, and I know a spot where there are lots of clams; I have gone there many times in the past, and Yumi will care for you in my absence. Enjoy the bathing while I'm gone." I have assured Miss Tami and gave Yumi an instruction to make the salve; mixing sulfur powder with aloe pulp apply it to Miss Tami's wounds, as well as on herself, and then I began to head down the path.

"Wait! The stick, Sister Taka—you must carry a stick before walking through that path." Yumi yelled at me, and her frightened voice stopped me in my tracks.

"Why, Yumi? Why the stick?"

"Sister Taka, have you forgotten about theHabu?"

"Oh—dear me, I had forgotten all about the habu. Thank you for reminding to me." I thanked Yumi, remembering the habu's lethal bite.

The habu is a small deadly venomous earthen-colored snake, about foot long, blends in with the surroundings and becomes invisible to an unsuspecting individual. The snake is aggressive in nature; it will strike at anything, and in the matter of few minutes the victim suffers paralysis of the nervous system. Eventually body functions shut down, and the victim succumbs to death. Moreover, no known antivenin exists. When a farmer is bitten by a habu, the only chance of survival is to sever his bitten finger or the toe at a crucial moment.

Armed with a long weeping willow branch, I proceed down a grassy path, beating the ground as I walked; Yumi assisted Tami onto her wheelchair, out of water and have her sits where warm soft breeze would dry her wet hair. Then gathered sulfur by scraping it off the rocks, mixed it with aloe pulp in a small tin bowl, and applied it to Tami's wounds, until covered the raw areas with a thin film. It was a rare lazy day; and relaxed in the warm summer afternoon as thoughts of war were far from minds.

"Any sign of Taka?" Miss Tami asked, and she was concerned about my long absence.

"Not yet Ma'am you need not worry, we've often forgotten about the passing time when we gathered clams for our family meal." Yumi relayed the experiences to calm Miss Tami's anxiety.

"Hello there, I'm back." I hollered from down below the hill.

"Miss Tami, I must help my sister carry the bucket, please excuse me for a moment." Yumi said, picked up a stick and beat the path as she hurried down to meet me.

I brought back a bucket full of huge oysters and clams, a sight to behold, but to cook them I had to improvise a cooking tool by bent a thin pliable willow branch on one end to make a circle to place a clam, and then threading another branch through the loop to hold up its weight. Then we watched the clams pop opened from the heat of steam, revealing mouthwatering morsels. We have consumed the clams and oysters as fast as clams were cooked until could not eat no more.

We have not had scrumptious meal like this, since when? A

thought were in our mind as we ate, and being blissfully content watching the huge orange sun melting down below the horizon, turning the sky with a spectacular blazing afterglow. The day was ending, and we must start back the darkness would fall soon. Quickly I bathed and put on the clean clothes Yumi has washed and dried. While putting everything Yumi washed and dried onto the wheelchair.

"We'll return tomorrow and spend the whole day." I said and carried Miss Tami on piggyback headed to the farmhouse.

"I've enjoyed myself very much. Thank you both, Taka, Yumi." Miss Tami's voice relayed her contentment.

Bathing daily in warm sulfur water, eating fresh seafood with a side order of sweet potatoes, and wild blackberries for a dessert, all of us have gradually regained health and strength. Miss Tami's wounds has healed to the point formed a thin skin, allowing her more mobility, but still extreme caution was needed to guard the newly formed skin. All was going well each day; however, I was beset by the thoughts to improve our living conditions, because already a chill in air after the sundown.

Winter will be there soon, bringing cold rain and skin curling icy winds, furthermore, our present attire would not keep us warm or in good health; the garments we wore had long passed the point of being threadbare, and one little pull would rip the fabric. I thought how to obtain dire need of the warm clothing and footwear, but having no clue as to how or where to obtain the needed items. Most urgently the farmhouse was not structurally secure; it would not seal out the approaching winter's cold and rain.

Days passed without the aid of calendar, but I surmised, if my memory serves correctly almost a month has passed since the bombing.

"Taka, I have not heard an air-raid siren."

"So have I, Miss Tami. I too have not heard I believe we are not at war?" Miss Tami mentioned one day. The enemy planes, but I am certain the war is still going on, ma'am, even though there is nothing more left to bomb. Please try not to think about it. Let us look forward to the day when peace will prevail upon us. I have relayed my thoughts to Miss Tami, convincing her to believe, and to believe in my own words.

One day, I brought out my an idea of relocating to, where would be more food and better housing because soon the bitter winter would bring cold rain which would pour in from all those holes in the roof, and the cold wind would blow in from the cracks in the wall. Going to the pond would be impossible in such weather, impossible to remain in this house.

Hearing my reason, Miss Tami and Yumi did not need any more convincing, but the question of "How and where to?" remained unanswered. But I mentioned of Shimabara, where my cousins lived, explaining about the foothills of the Shimabara Peninsula was graced with a mild weather all year around, and an abundance of crops to be had and many large fishes were caught every day from the bay. Miss Tami and Yumi did not know about Shimabara; but the picture I have painted was mighty inviting. Although a thought of "What if I am wrong about the plenty of food?" A smidgen of doubt nudged my mind, but I dismissed instantly and take a chance on going to Shimabara.

I have decided to inspect the estate once more before leaving, thinking, and "Maybe I've over looked something?" Running past the charred village still fogged in a foul odor, I have reached the estate's entrance gates, cautiously made my way up, only to find still remaining debris of catastrophe just as same as day we left the estate. I went searching for anything that could be of use, but found nothing panning my eyes around the ruined scene, and then I saw a damaged but still standing storage shed.

"Oh, the heaven above, please, I pray, not all is lost?" I said, running toward the shed, forgotten about being barefooted.

As I came upon the burnt shed, there was only a half of it still standing upright and looked as if it might collapse at any given moment. But maybe there is something in the shed that could be of use? I hoped and cautiously I entered. And then immediately saw the wooden trunk, which Yumi and me kept our belongings, knelt down and lifted its lid.

There on top was Mistress Shizuka's bejeweled black lacquer box, which I did not have the courage to destroy, secretly kept it from Mistress Shizuka. All the rest of contents were intact, and among them were the rare orchid perfume, sheaves of Yumi's beautifully embroidered silk fabrics, sewing needs, kimono robes Yumi has made, and my literary honor scrolls undamaged, I must keep them all I thought, lowered the trunk lid trying to figure a way to transport all that I found to the farmhouse, but could not think of an applicable solution.

And then a flash of thought suggesting; perhaps the shed could be used as a shelter? Encouraged by an inspiration, I began to inspect the interior more closely, but the damages were extensive and shed was unsafe. Not only unsafe, but also it would not withstand the winter's wrath. And then I saw a large gardener's cart covered under the fallen debris and to my delight, contained the gardener's entire equipment still loaded ready for work. Adding more to my delight, there were several pairs of pig-toed black rubber work boots, so named because the boot resembles a pig's hoof and commonly worn by the laborers and farmers. Five pairs of those boots were neatly lined up on the wall shelves. Also there were neatly folded undamaged work clothes.

Excited by findings, those could be of good use; I shouted with delight and immediately picked a pair of pig-toed boots and put them on, turning my foot this way and that to see how it looked. It made me laughed out loud to see my foot looking so hideously large, but the comfort of wearing footwear was a reward of it all.

Clearing the debris out of the way, I pulled the heavy cart out of the shed, pushing and pulling, and then unloaded the gardener's equipment to clear a space for the wooden chest, attempting to pull the chest up onto the cart, but the chest was too heavy for me to budge I have emptied all the trunk's contents and tried again, but even after being emptied the wooden chest was still too heavy, and I could not manage.

Determined to accomplish the task, I pushed the chest to back of cart, wrapped the gardener's rope around the wooden chest, and then lifted up the front end of the cart placed a piece a piece of charcoal crusted log underneath to hold it up. I then managed to push one end of the chest onto the cart, placed a rock behind it to hold it in place, pulled the rope taut and secured it to the cart's handlebar.

Repeating tirelessly, a little by little, I was able to push the trunk up on the cart. I then replaced contents back into the trunk, loaded some of the gardener's equipment, thinking those will be of use, back onto the cart and headed home, managed to pull the heavy cart eventually I returned to the farmhouse, totally exhausted, but elated with my finding.

Miss Tami and Yumi has been anxiously waiting for my return, and they saw me coming down the road pulling a cart, Yumi ran to give me help and greeted me with joy, she was beside herself to see the unexpected windfall. Even though, those equipments were mere gardening tools, but precious conduit to the Araki's grandiose days. Yumi and I have managed to bring the trunk into the house; and eagerly begun inspecting the contents. Immediately, Miss Tami noticed her mother's jewelry box and demanded an explanation. I have hesitated for a moment, but seeing Miss Tami's doubts in her eyes, I relayed the event took place with her mother.

"Are you telling me we are not poor?" Miss Tami said, unable to comprehend full magnitude of the circumstance.

"No, ma'am, we're not poor—afar from it." I said, removing the amulet from my neck, signaled Yumi to remove hers, and poured out the contents in front of her. A sight sparkling mound of the magnificent gems were mesmerizing, and Miss Tami scooped up a handful and watched them fall slowly from between her fingers, as if she was looking at an apparition.

"My mother—all these gems—how did she? I know they took everything. Grandfather and my father, didn't they know?" Miss Tami asked, jolted by the sight of gems.

"Yes, Miss Tami, perhaps the two men knew, but they kept quiet. You may have noticed your mother had an extraordinary extrasensory perception, and she was plagued by visions of the perilous dogmatism; even though she tried to rid her intrusive disquietude, but it grew stronger with the passing time. Continuing dogma alarmed your mother, and she has confided in us to be on guard to keep you from harm's way. Above all, she told us to conceal the gems in our possession; no one to find out, including you, ma'am. Your mother knew you'd be safer not knowing. You know now, we have an incredibly huge fortune; best not to breath a word of it even to ourselves. When the need arises, I will dispose of it discreetly to obtain the necessities. You need not worry, Miss Tami, we swore and gave your dear mother our pledge to protect and serve you," I have explained to Miss Tami.

"I know you have the best interest of my well being; I pray you'll be rewarded." Miss Tami said, sincerely expressed her gratitude.

One leisurely afternoon when we were at the hot spring pond, the sound of approaching planes invaded our senses, and heart skips a beat. Fearfully casting the eyes toward the direction of the sound, we spotted two fast approaching planes much larger than the Grumman bombers. I grabbed Miss Tami, and in one motion dove into the bush, threw my body over Miss Tami and held her in a bear hug waiting for the machinegun bullets to pierce our bodies, putting an end to our lives, while deafening sounds of the planes ripped the air. The planes flew over the field in low altitude; and I saw the pilots looking down at us hunched down in the bushes. Never in my life, had I felt blood-curling fear of seeing a huge plane flying low over my head, as though low enough for me to touch it.

The sound of the planes faded quickly as quiet returned in a matter of minute. I loosened death grip on Miss Tami and slowly looked up to see where those planes were, but the clear blue sky above did not give a hint as to anything was amiss; only the roaring sounds of the engines kept echoing in my head, as if the planes has never left.

"Look, Sister Taka. Look!" Yumi yelled, pointing her finger to the sky.

Against the bright mid afternoon sun, there were countless sheets of white leaflets floating down; those must have been dropped from the plane. Cautiously, Yumi picked one up but the words were written in English, and she was unable to read them and handed it to me.

"Miss Tami, please tell us what is written on this paper?" I asked.

It was a message to surrender, and read, GIVE UP WHILE YOU CAN, DON'T DELAY, SAVE YOURSELVES.

But to wave a white flag was admitting one's shameful defeat, failure, and betrayal to the Emperor. *"Never!"* people said, strong voice echoed in unison, but their hearts were silently crying, *"No more war."* Several more times leaflets were dropped, but the warnings fell on closed minds and eyes, and then came a final warning of, THE WARNING IS OVER. EVACUATE.

We took it seriously and decided to head west to the village of Shimabara, seeking safety where our parents must have gone. Yumi and I have gathered many clams, oysters and shrimp, and caught some fish; all of them were steamed and dried so it would keep during the journey. Also dug up more sweet potatoes as many as we could find, and Yumi gathered our belongings and packed for the trip ahead.

Before embarking on the journey west, I chose the pearl hair ornament and diamond studded gold brooch, which I have intended to sell, concealed in a rolled-up cloth and tied it to my waist under garment I wore, and headed east towards Fukuoka.

Fukuoka has encompassed the biggest and busiest seaport of northern Kyushu, also a center of the financial heart. There were big and small businesses and shops throughout the city; especially people were lured by four story high department stores. Families from surrounding counties would come to the big city of Fukouka for a weekend retreat.

My main concern was to find a jeweler and sell the gems at the highest going market price, hoping, there must be at least one jeweler who will gives me a good price?

After walking for two days, stopping overnight in an abandoned roadside house to sleep, I arrived in the outskirts of the city at dusk. But instead of a bustling city, there was an eerie silence and no bright city lights illuminating the night sky, no sounds of melody was heard; instead, a pungent burnt odor permeating in the air.

There were piles of rubble, some as high as a house, cautiously I proceeded further, but there was not a soul to be seen. Alone and fearful in the fast falling night, I have quickened my paces and headed for the railway station further east, hoping the building was still there. Luckily, the railway station was standing unharmed. Entering cautiously keeping my back against the wall, straining eyes to see if anyone was in the darkened waiting room, but nothing stirred, and I was alone.

Stealthily, I walked over to the wooden bench and sat down, as I did, my fatigue draining away and felt hungry, I took out few of the dried clams to eat, but I began to fall asleep suffering fatigue and sleep deprivation. I fought to stay awake, in fear of being robbed or even killed; I must stay awake to safe guard jewels. I told myself, but gave in to alluring sleep.

Although my body was suspended in sleep mode, my senses were alert detected a faint sound of unlike human footsteps. Instantly I sat up, looking for a weapon, a stick, stone, or anything I can get my hand on, but there was none. Holding the breath, I turned head slowly to get a glimpse of stealthily approaching stranger, trying to suppress the rapidly pounding loud sounds of my heart. The stranger, however, was a skin-and-bone black German shepherd; dragging his paws slowly he walked in front of me and sat down about two meters, five and half feet away without taking his eyes off me.

Instinctively I wanted to get up and run, but I could not move, so began to whisper, desperately trying not to rile the dog. *"P-poor dog, you're lost. Have you lost your master?"* My voice quivered and words were fragmented, but the dog seemed understood, and little by little he scooted closer and settled himself under the bench where I was sitting, which made me very nervous, but realizing the dog seems not a threat I kept talking. *"You must be hungry; I will share my food with you."* I said, put the few clams in my palm and slowly lowered hand to dog.

As hungry as the dog must have been, he picked one clam at a time from my hand; and he ate with a mannerly behavior while drooled on my palm, and then proceed to lick away every bit of taste left on my hand, and then he laid down, fall fast to sleep.

The dog's not a threat. I told myself, and trying to stay awake to protect gem, though I woke at daybreak. Realizing I was sleep, instantly my hand went to the cloth holding the gems, around my waist, and I made certain the gems were still in my possession, I walked out from the railway station.

The dawn's light has revealed the horrible graveyard of once prosperous and busy city, and had the many shops, restaurants, and hotels for travelers; but there was nothing but heaps and heaps of debris spread out in front of train station. I was lost as to find any establishment, which may have escaped the fiery destruction, but I could not see any near or the far. Hopelessly dismayed, I could not gather a thought where to go from here. There must be someone, but where? I was asking myself, while looking around to detect any sign of people. And then I saw a thin stream of smoke rising not too far away. *"Someone's there!"* I said out loud and headed straight toward the smoke, not realizing the German shepherd was following few yards back.

Trekking through and over the charred masses of debris, I headed toward the smoke, but the rising smoke was further away than it appeared. Then I saw a smoke rising from under a partially intact bridge, once straddled over flowing river in the middle of the city, but few people were huddled around a small fire. They turned to stare at an approaching stranger, with a dog. *"Please, don't be alarmed. I'm only passing through, and the dog is harmless."* I said, stopped just within an earshot of them to ease their tension.

"What d' ya want, we have nothing to share…" A woman said in no uncertain term, but her voice was weak and thin.

"I'm not looking for a handout—only an information, ma'am," I asked. But they were still cautious, looking at each other with their guard up.

"Is there a marketplace I can buy some food?" I asked, but no one responded; they only stared at me with a blank expression. I waited for a moment, but no one spoke, so turned to leave.

"Ma'am, wait—we didn't mean to be rude, but as you can see none of us is in any mood for company. We've been through a hell— just look around you. We've lost everything and don't know how to make it through today, tomorrow, and after that?" A man spoke with disheartened voice, informed me that he and the others had not eaten for some time. "The market you've asked for exists; it used to be Iwataya department store, but it's a black market now and squatters' haven. Be cautious and protect yourself," man advised.

I thanked the man and headed out, picking my way through more debris, being careful to avoid sharp objects and protruding rusted nails; while the shepherd led the way, he sensed where the hidden dangers were. The Iwataya department, once a main attraction of city has came into view, and the shepherd halted staring in the direction of the building, sniffing the air to assess the situation, and then he gave a small bark as his signal of approval and the dog and I have proceeded forward.

Chapter 6: Black Market

In its heyday, when people lived each day in peace, the Iwataya department store was the elite place to shop; they made plans well in advance to come to the city and spend a day at the Iwataya, mingling among the affluent sophisticated ladies of high social standing. And upon returning home, they told their neighbors, *"I've been to the Iwataya,"* as if a member of the high society.

It was the Mistress Shizuka's favorite place to shop, and often she came to see the latest designer fashions, domestic and foreign. I always accompanied Mistress to the Iwataya, and while the mistress and her acquaintances were enjoying each other's company, without the usual social formality, I went about enjoyed browsing and looking at the beautiful jewelry shining in a glass case under a light, as well as the many pretty kimonos.

Today, there were no tall colorful banners bearing the name Iwataya lining the front entrance, and no stream of people going in and coming out carrying packages. I stood and stared at the building, once held a dream of many wishful people, was covered with black soot smeared by smoke and fire standing as if a ghost amongst the debris.

I recalled the days of grandeur in solace, remembering how I have enjoyed the open-air teahouse on the rooftop, viewing the exotic tropical birds in the natural setting of a large aviary, while savoring sushi and sipping hot tea, watching the many colorful birds in awe. Sadly all those birds were gone, the teahouse was in shambles, and only a ruin left to reminds me of the time of peace long ago.

Walking into the building, there were wall-to-wall people squatted on the bare concrete floor; an each claimed a small space as their own as only salvation, stripped of all their earthly goods, even down to the soul, and the hopes for the future were none. I threaded my way carefully, in between them while their stinging indignant, but blank eyes staring has stung dog and me. And we have carefully traipsed through a narrow space, not to step on any of their belonging.

"Another squatter, even got a dog." Their thought emanated from eyes, and we came upon a man claiming an intrusively large space, had a display table covered with colorful eye-catching goods, such as cheap trinkets and ready-to-eat food, and put-on smile to lure any customers who may have something to sell, and he would pay a minimal amount for their belongings, which were the conduits to their happier days, they held on to as long as they could, until hunger drove them to sell the precious mementos and use the money to buy food.

I found a small space, for the dog and me, and for tonight we have to sleep hungry on the concrete floor, but tomorrow I must find a buyer for the jewels. *"Sleep well. You've been a great companion and protector. I know you are hungry—we both are. I'll have some food for us tomorrow."* I whispered, stroking the shepherd lying next to me. I was trying to think of a name for him, but sleep soon claimed us tired twosome in a pungent unwashed body odor and the noises.

Sounds of clattering and talking voices penetrated into my sleeping brain, and I began to come to from a coma, as the sounds has woke me gotten louder, though took a moment or two before I was wake enough to comprehends where I was, but when I saw the black shepherd quietly sitting by me my mind instantly cleared. *"Come, Tenshi,"* I called. At that moment how the name Tenshi (an Angel) suited the shepherd, and the dog responded to his new name as if he knew it all along.

Tenshi and I have made our way, ignoring all those squatters staring and whispering something to each other, as made our way toward the man sitting on a fancy red-and-gold silk brocade settee, an unusual luxury in such miserable gloomy surroundings. I know that man, I thought, and trying to recall, where have I seen him before? Then I remembered the incident happened thirteen years ago shot through my brain, reminding me of a life altering day.

Although his appearance has changed by the passing years, an old man sitting on the fancy settee was the same man my father has tried to sell Yumi and me as a prostitute; his unmistakable an image of being well fed and large figure was ingrained in my brain all those years. I moved in closer to have a good look at the man sitting behind the table, and it was no mistake he was the one who came to the house riding in a shiny rickshaw. The long-ago incident came back as brought flood of memories horrified me.

"You got something to sell? Maybe want to buy my pretty trinkets?" The man spoke, and I was jolted by his voice, pulled back my wandering mind to the present.

"Oh—aah—yes, sir, I do have some important merchandise;

however, I fear you'll not be able to meet my asking price. Perhaps you know of someone who can?" I stated with an air of superiority, but the pretence of it caused my heart to beat hard, and an extreme hunger has induced lightheadedness, and I began to faint.

Quickly, the men grabbed hold of me and led into his compound, where I sat on his settee and have some of his water to drink. I regained a bit of strength from water, while Tenshi never took his eyes off the man. I poured a little water into my palm for Tenshi and then hesitantly asked for some food, explaining I have not eaten since yesterday, and apologizing for being an onus.

"Woman, you are audacious! First, you said I don't have enough money to pay for your trinket, and then, out of the goodness of my heart, I let you sit on my settee and gave you water. Now you have the gall asking me to feed you?" The man was appalled by my bold request; however, looking at my famished appearance, he was aware that I needed nourishment. So against his better judgment, he gave me a part of his meal and more water. I shared food and water with Tenshi, and both of us has quickly consumed, and I thanked the man for his generosity and stood up to leave.

"Wait—I understand that you have something to sell?" The man asked; but judging by my appearance, he doubted I had anything of value, although his curiosity got the best of him and asked to see it. First I was apprehensive about showing the gems to a man, who is no doubt without conscious takes an advantage of destitute people, but after given a thought, and I have decided perhaps this man may be able to handle the transaction.

"A second thought, you may, sir. However, the viewing must be done discreetly." I have emphasized. And that request heightened the man's curiosity even more. Furthermore, I have demanded it for your eyes only, so much so that he simply had to see it.

"But with one condition, sir: my dog must accompany you at

all time." I have stipulated, and the man agreed, but he was apprehensive to be in such close proximity with a big dog.

Upon both us has agreed to the condition, I went into an enclosure, removed the sash from my waist took out the folded cloth, and I held the exquisite gold, diamonds, and pearls in the palm of my hand, looked at the sparking gems, even in an enclosed darkroom. *"Stay here and guard these jewels."* I commanded Tenshi, and left him in the enclosure, gestured the man to inspect the jewels.

Entering the enclosure, man was acutely aware of the big dog, doubting he would not find anything of value. A minute passed, then two, and then three more minutes, while a heavy silence hung behind the enclosure. I felt uneasy, and stood up to check what was keeping him. Just then a hand parted the curtain and the man emerged with Tenshi close behind. The look on his flushed face clearly expressed disbelief of what he saw.

"Where did you get this jewelry—did you steal it?" The man asked in an accusatory manner, because some expensive jewelry has been found under a burnt house, and this man has bought such jewelries in a past.

"No, sir, I did not steal the jewels. Those jewels were placed in my care by the grand mistress." I have stated with a forceful disposition.

"I see," the man said still had an air of unconvinced. *"However, I can well imagine the asking price. Tell me the numbers you have in mind?"* He asked.

I had to come up with the sum quickly, but having no idea of the gems' actual worth.

"A million yen. Not a yen less, sir," boldly I have stated concealing my hard beating heart, holding breath, and my eyes focused directly on his face.

"Uuuum one million yen! That's a great deal of money, although I must admit, the jewels are magnificent and there is not a flaw among them. Okay, it's a deal." The man slapped his knee to confirm. And that moment I exhaled, acting nonchalant as breathed a sigh of relief. In 1950, beginning of the occupation, a dollar was an equal to three hundred sixty Japanese yen.

"I thank you for your agreement, and also may I appeal to you for your kindness?"

"What that might be?" He asked.

"May I have enough food to last for two days? It's for my return trip, sir—as many rice cakes as you can give me, and dried fish I can eat without cooking, also a canteen of drinking water, please." I asked.

"Woman! You drive a hard bargain, but I will comply. I must take a short leave of absence; but I will be back in about two hours. You stay here and take care of my shop until I return." The man said left the premises.

I have secured the jewels around my waist again, and waited for the man to return, but the promised time came and went and nights had fallen and still no sign of the man.

Finally, after several hours have passed, the man returned with the money and a large parcel that has contained the items, but before the exchange took place, I have demanded to count the money. The man was appalled at not being trusted by the likes of me, knowing he had been up-front in dealing from the beginning, but having no other choice he obliged. I counted the money carefully and found it was all there. And then removed the sash from my waist, lifted a folded edge just enough for the man to see the jewels and handed it over to him.

"Many thanks for your swiftness in dealing with me. We, however, never introduced ourselves; but it is in our best interest to

part as strangers. You're a man with heart, sir—not at all what I have imagined. May the good fortune come your way?" I said and thanked him bowed deeply.

"Just a moment, I take it that you know me?" The man asked with a puzzled look on his face.

"Many pardons sir. However; with due respect, I decline to answer your question." I have stated, and bowed again left quickly with Tenshi.

Before returning home, I have managed to purchase some expensive black market goods, such as matches, salt, tissue, and twelve pounds—four and half kilo of rice, all illegal items I carried on my shoulder and headed for the railway station to stay the night.

Up at sunrise, Tenshi and I have shared few rice cakes and some water before we begun our arduous trek back home, though I was unaware of having a smile on my face, thinking of sharing the good news with Tami and Yumi. Although acutely aware of having a large sum of money in my possession, but I felt confident and secure, knowing Tenshi would deter any attempt robbery.

Home at last after a long absence, I have unfolded the details of my trip to the girls, leading them through the devastated city of Fukuoka, and telling them how by chance I found a man from the past knew him only by a sight, though finding him has made my mission successful. In addition, Tenshi and I have found each other, and he became trusted companions; moreover, Tenshi was a heaven-sent to protect the girls and me.

Chapter 7: Fallen Country

Yumi had been preparing as much food as she could for the long trip ahead to the village of Shimabara; walking an entire distant, the reason being, all the public transportation was discontinued, and fuel that has needed to run were routed to the war front where needs were urgent.

Everything was ready and it was time for us to leave, but I thought it was in a best interest to leave wooden chest behind, reluctantly I did to avoid a possible attempted robbery. Because the chest would appear we had something of value, we have removed all the contents from the chest, Yumi and I folded flat, made a makeshift futon for Miss Tami, laid it on a top of the three hundred thousand yen also wrapped in our raggedy attires.

The jewelry box was wrapped in rags, makeshift pillow for Miss Tami, and dried foods were wrapped in a rag tied to the underside of cart, and the concealments worked out well, and those folded raggedy clothing was our only valued belonging.

Checking the house once more, Yumi and I have bid a silent farewell to the old farmhouse, through our tear-blurred eyes, knowing we may never see it again, and walked away as though being torn apart from mother's warm bosom, it was in our best interest to leave the house that was not able to seal out the winter's ire and cold wind: And then battering icy rain would pour in through the dilapidated walls and holes on the roof.

Miss Tami was securely seated on the makeshift futon, we begun trekking away from the old farmhouse, and Tenshi was leading the way. Passing by the ruined village, we have hastened strides to avoid foul odor still hanging in the air.

As we approached the Araki estate, immediately I noticed the driveway's gates were open, and weeds growing intrusively covering over the gates and walkway. Miss Tami turned her face away; she was unable to look at the entranceway in such disrepair. I ran quickly to pull the weeds away and close the gates, to deter any scavengers from entering the estate and resumed journey northward, heading to the northern shore of Ariake Bay to turn south, which lays between Shimabara and western shore of Fukuoka.

Tenshi was on guard, running in front or following in behind; sometimes he would jump up on the cart, laid next to Miss Tami and two of them napped together, cradled by the cart's rocking motion.

Rounding the northern shore of Ariake Bay, we head south advanced further, when we all noticed a change of scenery in the countryside. There were lush green fields covered with masses of pink clover flowers, and the sparkling leaves on trees casting shades here and there under the bright sun, and it has created as though Monet's best work of an art.

High in the blue sky there was a pair of haws gliding over the field, looking for a prey, recreating a picture of long ago vision.

Resuming trek south, we came to an old towering persimmon

tree loaded with the sweet ripened fruits, a rare treat we have not had for so long, and many ripened fruits were fallen on the ground. We decided to camp under the tree for the night, parked the cart in the shade of the tree and prepared a spot for Miss Tami to rest.

Yumi and I have broiled salt-cured fish and dried squids over a small campfire and after the meal, all of us savored soft and sweet persimmons, even Tenshi ate the persimmons that had fallen on the ground. Being satisfied and comfortable, we stretched out on the thick grass under the tree, and Tenshi lie under the cart to rest. All of us fall fast asleep and threat of the war seemed far away.

Pioneers have settled here, in the primordial pristine countryside centuries ago, and to sustain themselves grew and harvest abundance of crops from rich volcanic soil. Their chickens laid many eggs, cows produced abundance of milk, and the men hunted wild game such as rabbits, wild boars, and pheasants as their valued stock of foods, and the settlers lived comfortably. No one had a radio or newspaper in this remote legion; seldom passing travelers has told the news if any.

Then I had sudden an inspiration and it waken me from a rare moment of serenity, and I did about face. *"Miss Tami, do you know what month this is?"* I asked, and I am sure my face was beaming, and my eyes must have sparkling.

"No, I hadn't kept track of the passing months. Why?" Miss Tami answered with question, and she asked. *"How old are you?"*

"I don't rightly know, ma'am. I remember being fifteen when I came to the estate, and Yumi was nine then, so I must be twenty-eight, and that makes Yumi twenty-two. It's a foreign feeling to think about birthdays, when we should be thinking about our survival, but the uncertain future does not have a threatening effect on me, as do to others. Perhaps we are still young enough not to burden with such matter." I answered.

"I hope you are right about your assumption, and having this conversation made me believe there are good things waiting in our future. I am not fearful as much not having my parents." Miss Tami said, and for the first time since the bombing, the expression on her face showed signs of glad tidings.

The next morning, Yumi and I picked more ripened persimmons and savored the soft and sweet delicacy; an unexpected gift of nature at its best, and we could not eat any more. Yumi picked more persimmons for the journey ahead, and we resumed the trek south.

Came upon farmers working in the field, and an old straw-thatched house was short distance away. I stopped to talk to the woman who was tilling the field.

"Excuse me, ma'am. Please, we've been on the road for three days and in need of food and water; as you can see we have a sick young lady." I have informed the woman, and she dropped her shovel and came running to see Miss Tami, who was lying on the cart.

"She's been burnt badly. How did this happened?" the woman asked, aghast at the sight of her wounds.

"Our village was burnt to the ground by the bombing, and many have perished, but luckily we were able to escape with our lives and found an empty old farmhouse to sheltered ourselves, but the task of obtaining our necessary staples became more difficult with each passing day. We are on our way to find my distant relatives who live in the village of Shimabara, where I hear the food is plentiful. I'm hoping to find them, because it may be our only chance of survival," I have explained to her.

"Yes, I heard about the war, but we didn't know it was still going on." the farmer's wife said, and invited us to stay the night at their house.

While the evening meal was being prepared, I help to bathe

Miss Tami and put clean garments on and sat her in the wheelchair to relax and enjoy the moment.

Tami felt farmer's wife's staring at her with a prying curiosity. Amazing! She thought to herself, seeing the chair with such big wheels. And they treat the young girl as if someone very important, and called her Miss Tami; and that dog, he's more of a human than just a dog. Who are these people? They look poor, but acted like the royalty. Mystified, the farmer's wife sipped her tea nervously, but no longer could she suppress her curiosity.

"Ma'am, was the meal satisfactory?" farmer's wife asked, desperately wanting to start a conversation.

"Yes, thank you very much. It's been a long time since we had a real home-cooked meal," Miss Tami answered. And then I joined in the conversation.

"I can't even remember when I cooked a meal for the family." I said, staring into a cup of hot tea. *"It's a miracle we're still alive."* I murmured, as a fragrance of green tea brought back the memories of the Araki's heyday.

"Forgive me, ma'am, I did not mean to pry." The farmer's wife apologized.

"Please, you needn't apologize, we're grateful for you and your husband. You must be wondering who we are?" I said, began to explain the reason for going to the village of Shimabara. *"I'm hoping to find my distant relatives, and I believe my parents too have gone there to escape the air raids. I must find them; it's our only chance of survival, and we will depart an early tomorrow morning."*

The aroma of the morning meal began drifting in the air I knew the farmer's day starts out early, but this morning a bitter memory arose from the aroma of miso soup. At an age of five, every morning before dawn, I was pulled out from thin futon by my father and went to work in a field, along side of my brothers and the father.

Mother stayed at home to do her chores, starting a fire in the cooking pit to prepare the morning meal, and carrying baby on her back. When the sun arose it was time to go home and eat. This was the only heartening time of the day for me, having steamed rice and miso soup, which gave me the strength I needed to work until nightfall.

Next morning, we were ready to leave, when the farmer's wife brought a large satchel full of food she had prepared for us, along with a jug of cold well water to drink. This was an unexpected kind gesture by the farmer couple.

Girls and I have expressed our gratitude, and I placed the satchel and water on the cart, and I returned with a piece of folded tissue paper containing one thousand yen, which I have placed in the farmer's hand and said. *"We owe a debt of gratitude to you and your wife; this is a small token of our gratitude for all you've done for us."*

"Ohhh, it was nothing; we've enjoyed your company, y'all come back again. We get mighty lonesome around here not having children and all. Ma'am, you don't have to pay us, but please stop by to see us when y'all can." Farmer said and tried to give back the folded tissue, but he was up against my unyielding refusal to take back the gift of thanks.

Reluctantly farmer accepted it with his gratitude, and after sending the girls on their way, the farmer and his wife unfolded the tissue, and to their surprise there was 1,000-yen bill. Seeing such large sum of money, they have hustled to catch the girls and return the money, but the visitors were long gone.

A sound of gentle lapping waves reached into Tami's dream self, and slowly she began to wake, but Tami's lagging mind was still projecting an image of a little child holding onto her grandfather's hand strolling in the garden. A pair of peacocks spread opens huge iridescent tail feathers like big fans—magic to the child's eyes, Miss Tami let out a squeal and delighted laughter; she turned around to see if Yumi and I saw it too.

Fully awake, Tami was doused with the cold reality of life's pitfalls, *"Mama!"* Miss Tami whispered, blinking off her brimming tears.

"Good morning, ma'am. Hot water for your morning toiletry is ready, and your breakfast will be served shortly." Yumi announced from other side of the closed shoji.

Every morning, Tami awoke to the cruel reality of living in a barn at a small fishing village, where they have been for the past five months. But the village was unaffected by the changing era; still a primordial place, the villagers went fishing, and farmers worked in their patch of field just as their forefathers has done, still using the primitive oxen-driven equipment, which has handed down from their elders. Few of the villagers had an old radio, but newspapers were scarce; moreover, they have no need for those modern technologies.

I have searched for my parents, but unsuccessful, and I doubt that they even came here, so reluctantly I gave it up.

After the morning meal, I have assisted Miss Tami into the wheelchair and every morning, three of us went for our daily walk, never failed to attract curious onlookers no matter how many times they saw us, and in their full view I maneuvered the wheelchair carefully through the uneven narrow paths of farm field to the seashore, and strolling along the water's edge enjoying a cool sea-scented breeze, while Tenshi following behind. But the cool morning temperature began to rise, their faces were moistened with perspiration, and Tenshi was panting to cool himself. The day was the clear summer morning of August the ninth, 1945.

"Taka, I am getting hot. Let us go back." Miss Tami said, feeling uncomfortable. Obliging her at once and I turned the wheelchair around to head back. At that instant, we saw a black line extending above the top of the Unzen mountain range, east to west.

Odd? I thought, seen the unusual sight, and Tami and Yumi too were staring at the ominous black line that was slowly rising yet higher as though storm was coming. However, in this region, the storms approach from the southerly direction, accompanied by dark rain clouds, blowing in fast over the bay. Never in metrological history had a huge coal-black cloud arisen from behind the northern mountain range.

People ran out in the street, all staring fearfully at the huge black cloud rising higher and higher, and it began to cove r the sun as the entire northern half and turned the sky black as an eclipse, as the night had fallen at midmorning, changing the bright sun into a bloody red. No one knows what was happening.

"Look!" A man shouted pointing his finger to a small patch of clear southern sky; where there were two shiny silver planes at high altitude heading south and quickly disappeared into the clouds.

"That was B-29s." someone yelled knowledgeably recognizing the two silvery planes. People were puzzled by the appearance and disappearance of the B-29s, which did not drop the bombs as everyone was expecting. On that day, planes dropped the atomic bomb on the city of Nagasaki, unaware of its power would incinerates and blow off an entire city from face of earth.

We were frightened by the unexplainable horror, as I pushed the wheelchair in dark to reach our safety of the shack. In a darkened room, breathless and shaking with fear huddled together and we waited for imminent end to our lives and the world. Quiet—too quiet—not a sound of chirping birds, people talking, clutter of farmers' cartwheels, and cows mooing in the distance—all were muted.

Rained the next day, and the villagers were horrified to see the gray rain fell from sky. Fearfully they waited for the gray rain to stop, hiding in their house keeping an eye on Mount Unzen for any sign of another black cloud.

It's rained the next three days, and grey rain turned clear droplets the villagers breathed a sigh of relief, begun emerging from their houses, expecting more of unexplainable occurrence. But nothing happened and slowly one by one they returned to their daily chores, fishing and tending their fields; all thanked the Buddha for his grace and resumed their uncomplicated lives, never dreamt to the sudden horrifying intrusion would soon befalls and upheaval their lives.

The day the sun shed bloody tears, and the morning turned to a night, an experimental atomic bomb was dropped on the city of Nagasaki, due west of the Shimabara Peninsula where Mount Unzen stood in the center. Nagasaki was known to the world over, as a colorful modern city, bustling with exotic European culture and old Japanese culture existing in harmony. Also it was the birthplace of Madam Butterfly, and the famed composer Giacomo Puccini had written the famous opera Madama Butterfly, and gave the world a beautiful heroine in love, and her sad life story.

For centuries only in Nagasaki, European culture and hardcore Japanese feudalistic culture has coexisted in harmony, along with Buddhism and Shintoism. But the pernicious atomic bomb had annihilated the unique medley of foreign and Japanese lives in the city of Nagasaki. Lamentably, the bomb destroyed their priceless artworks.

The American scientists knew they created a powerful bomb, but did not have a clue as to the unimaginable magnitude of its destructive power, and conferred with the president about testing the bomb prior to dropping it on their enemy, and received his go-ahead to target Japan. Later they realized, not only they have created a monster, but also it had fatal side effects affecting human lives for the many years thereafter. Dropping the atomic bombs opened Pandora's Box, releasing microscopic poison particles of radioactive wastes, were carried away by wind currents to other geographical areas, poisoning everything in its path and ultimately killing people who came in contact.

The B-29, Super fortress bomber Enola Gay, had flown at low altitude to drop the first bomb on the city of Hiroshima, when the bomb was detonated, its explosion shook the huge B-29 on their return flight in high altitude, and the pilots saw the blinding flash of white light covering the city's radius. Two days later, a second atomic bomb was dropped on Nagasaki.

That fateful morning of August the ninth, in the blink of an eye, an explosion had seared the entire city of Nagasaki and its people into ashes. The heat of the explosion had surpassed one million degrees Fahrenheit, and created a huge fire dome vacuumed billions tons of ashes and debris, up into the stratosphere, with the wind velocity of 1,000 miles per hour sucked up the ashes and debris, grew into a giant mushroom cloud left the city of Nagashaki as though it has never existed.

"Water! Please, water!" "Help, help me." "Mama, help me, please, help me." The victims begged and cried for help, sitting amongst the dead, but only scratchy hisses came from their parched throats. Cooked skin hung melted off a man's body, draped hideously over a belt that has held his trousers, gruesomely naked and in excruciating pain, he knew something horrible has happened, but he did not have a clue as to what hit him... dragging his skin, a part still attached to the soles of his feet.

None of the victims knew what has happened. Men were going to the train station; wives were going to the market, some carrying her baby on her back, when doused by a blinding white flash, accompanied with high heat.

They crawled desperately toward the river, driven by unbearable thirst and, pain, but the bodies never moved under the glaring heat of the August sun while their body decomposed alive laden with maggots. Ironically their minds remained clear and alert, felt every pain, heard others' cries, and voice of cry for help was nothing more than a scratchy hiss until the victim drew a last breath two weeks later.

Some of the survivors appeared uninjured, but later they developed cancers like leukemia, tumors, and melanoma, which terminated their lives. And the offspring of appeared unscathed, were born hideously deformed: Mercifully those babies died before their first birthday.

On August 14, 1945, Japan fell to its knees; an unconditionally surrendered to the General MacArthur, signed peace treaty on board of the battleship Missouri, with their heads hung in shame. For the first time in history of Japan, atomic bomb has brought down once boasted *"we are the unbeatable."* General Tojo has pursued, driven by his axis of avarice, relentlessly to possess power over the world, which begun WWII, and he has Willfully sacrificed many young Japanese lives, as well as the lives of many young Americans who were called to duty to protect the defenseless countries. In an end General Tojo was indicted as a war criminal, along with his associates, and sentenced to death by hanging.

The residents of Shimabara knew nothing of what has happened to the city of Nagasaki, until the burnt victims of the bomb began to descend upon the unsuspecting people of the village. They have escaped from the barren desert of death and walked miles to seek refuge in a quaint village of Shimabara, which turned into chaos. And through the refugees, the villagers finally learned what has happened on that strange day when the sun shed bloody tears.

"Shinto God is angry!" a crazed old man stood in the street, shouting at an every passerby.

"End of the world is coming," another shouted with conviction.

"Honorable Buddha can't save us now." women cried, seeing all those horribly burnt people, disfigured, covered with caked-on dried blood and dirt, worst of all had maggots teeming in open wounds oozing with pus all were begging for food and water, the sight of it frightened villagers senseless.

Sympathetic villagers gave as much help as they could, but feeding them became impossible, as the immigrating refugees increased by an hour; they squatted in the fields, down in the ditches lining the side of the road, and wherever a space could be had.

Incredibly all those refugees have walked away from Nagasaki, carrying injured loved ones on their backs, even though they themselves were injured, but having no choice, they sat by their loved ones and simply waited for an inevitable death to come swiftly, and putting an end to their agonizing life on earth. But the merciful death they wished for did not come quickly; all died slowly one by one where they sat.

Voluntarily, the villagers removed decaying corpses and set them on a pyre, and its smoke with the noxious fumes of burning flesh drifted into the village, caused the villagers to become ill. It has been almost a month since all those injured refugees came into the village, and the situation was intolerable.

Lately I thought seriously about returning to the farmhouse, and I brought up the subject to Tami and Yumi, and they emphatically agreed. I am aware only hardship awaits us, but we'll have a house built, a small one perhaps, and we'll make do until we are able to have a larger one. Miss Tami suggested, a thought brought on by her innocent mind, and she smiled jubilantly.

I had no idea where to find the building supplies, or whom I could ask for help, but assuring Miss Tami that the building her house was a top priority on the list.

Yumi and I have prepared foods for our trip back and concealed the money in the same manner as I did previously, while the Miss Tami herself rendered helping hands by folding belongings readying for tomorrow's departure. Tenshi knew something was up; he was all excited, running around Yumi and me busily loading the cart, and then after the tasks were done, he jumped up on the cart and stayed there throughout the night, and early the next morning we headed out.

As we have distanced ourselves from the village, the stench of smoke faded as we continued northward, and we recognized the landscape in the vicinity of the farmhouse. Recalling the farmer couple welcomed three strangers and treated them with kindness. We decided to visit with them and stay for the night. Approaching closer the farmer couple saw us coming, and they came running to greet, happy to have unexpected reunion and a chance to celebrate the visit together.

We had so much to tell them about our life in the quiet fishing village of Shimabara; also told them about the unimaginable assault of calamity, which literally turned the village and the world upside down, throwing the villagers into a cauldron of chaos. Also I told the story of the atomic bomb dropped on the city of Nagasaki, wiping the city off the face of the earth. And survivors fled, and finding their way to the village of Shimabara, thus the villagers were inundated with the horribly wounded victims to care for, but most of them died one by one where they sat.

Hearing the devastating news, the farmer and his wife shed tears of sympathy, and they lit the candles and incenses for the deceased and prayed for them to rest in peace; and for those who were still suffering, we asked the Buddha to end their agony by a swift and merciful death.

After a night's rest and hearty morning meal, the girls bid farewell to the couple once again, but before leaving Taka handed another thousand-yen bill to the host farmer as a token of their appreciation.

"Miss, please, this is too much money; in fact we still have the one-thousand-yen bill you gave us. This is too much money, please, ma'am—surely you'll need this money." The farmer insisted, trying to return the money he held in his shaking hand.

"Sir, please keep the money. Contrary to our appearances, we are not paupers, and furthermore, the kindness you and your wife have lavished upon us is priceless. Please, sir, this is only a small token of our appreciation; however, be advised not to breathe a word of this to anyone, especially of whom you've received this money from; I'm safeguarding ourselves as well as of yours." I said to persuade farmer.

"I understand, ma'am, and we'll abide by your wish." The farmer gave his word, realizing the possible consequences. The farmer's wife packed more ready-to-eat foods for the girls and sent them on their way.

Sights of familiar landmarks came into view in the distance, and as we approached closer we were at the Araki estate gates. The gates were closed just as I left them, but the profusely overgrown bushes and weeds had overtaken the driveway. I stood in front of the gates; maybe the bomb shelter is livable? Decided to inspect the estate, pushed the way through heavy growth, and Tenshi came along hoping to find a meal, but I found the estate ground had been completely taken over by more of the wildly growing weeds and bushes concealing the debris. Unfortunately the bomb shelter has turned into a foul-smelling cesspool, full of mosquitoes and slimy crawling inhabitants.

What will I do now? I thought, staring at the blackened stagnant water, did not heard the strange sounds of drone was permeating from within the bomb shelter, and then before I realized, in a mere moment, stinging vermin's covered my body, drawn by the human body odor. I ran slapping and brushing the mosquitoes headed for the storage shed, but the damaged structure has crashed to the ground. Dismayed, I stood among the ruins, looking around to see if anything could be used as a livable habitat, but nothing appeared feasible and the situation seemed hopeless, my thoughts ran rampant; trying to figure a solution but my mind went blank; mindlessly following Tenshi chasing something running around among the weeds.

The farmhouse! A sudden thought struck, *"Please let it be still standing."* I said, voicing my thought out loud, excited by an inspiration. and I called, *"Come, Tenshi, we must go."* He came running out from behind the bushes, ran to Yumi and Miss Tami long before I caught up with him, and I relayed my finding. *"We'll go back to the farmhouse if it's still there—but if not; we'll pitch a tent by the hot spring pond so we can bathe at any time as we please. We'll not let you down, Miss Tami; I'll find away to build a house for you."* I said, putting on a cheerful front.

"You know best." Miss Tami said, more to herself, concealing her disappointment.

As we were passing through the village, there was no foul

odor, but instead few small crude shacks had been built with salvaged debris, and incredibly few hibiscus have sprouted from under the ashes, and its blossoms has created a stark contrast of red and yellow flowers against heaps of blackened debris.

"How lovely!" Miss Tami exclaimed.

"Indeed, ma'am, I've never dreamt those flowers would come back," I agreed in amazement.

There was an old woman watching us, and our big dog from a nearby hut, but as we were passing on by, she came hurrying toward us.

"Miss—please, wait a moment." the woman called out, being curious, we stopped and waited. *"Miss, wait, aren't you the servants of the Araki family?"* she asked.

"Yes, we are, and this young lady is the family's only survivor, Miss Tami Araki."

"Pleased to make your acquaintance, I escaped the fire, but everybody died—my family, their family, and all dead." The woman was babbling began to sob.

"I am very sorry about your family, ma'am. Everything's gone—everything," She said between sobs.

"Yes, all of us lost everything, but we have survived, we must go on." I said trying to encourage her.

"A man came by and said he was an Araki servant; he asked if any of you have survived. I told him that all died; I didn't know—very sorry. But if he comes by again, I will tell him you are alive and well. This is the least I can do to repay Senior Araki for his kindness; he was a very generous man and he helped us villagers in time of need. May he rest in peace? I wish you all well." An old woman said and bowed deeply.

"Perhaps there is something you can do for us?" I asked.

"Ma'am, anything I can do, please tell me." She said.

"If you see that servant again, inform him that I wish to recruit all the former servants. We're planning to build a house for our Miss Tami and ourselves. Have him report to me; he can find us at an old farmhouse not far south of here," I have specified.

The farmhouse was still standing, but barely, and it needed a good cleaning inside and out. Immediately Yumi and I got down to the task of clearing overgrown bushes, but saving the wild chrysanthemums, its smoke produces citronella.

While the house was being fumigated, we headed out to the hot spring pond to enjoy the pleasure of taken a hot bath; even Tenshi was splashing about in a warm stream and then dashed off to hunt for his meal.

I prepared delicious oysters and clams, broiling them over an open fire, and then we all enjoyed the gifts from the sea, a meal fit for the Emperor. The huge descending sun was just above the horizon, and it was time to head back; by now the house must be free of undesirable habitants, especially snakes. Even though the dilapidated farmhouse appeared barely able to stand, but at the time of need, it stood upright like an old soldier ready to be of service.

The night sky was pitch dark and full of stars, and the insects were orchestrating a one-of-a-kind symphony, creating an enchanting lullaby that seduced Tami and Yumi into a dream world. But I was too keyed up, tossed and turned under the weight of my responsibilities, thinking about the impossible task of building a house. Where do I begin? Where am I to find the lumber, and men to do the work? How? Where? My mind was stuck in a groove going around in a circle.

Awoke at the dawn, realizing I had been asleep, and quietly went out into the cool misty air of an early morning and breathed in the sweet taste of cool fresh air, which cleared my foggy head and enabled me to organize my thoughts.

Tenshi followed me out, running off into a field to hunt for his prey. I watched the black dog appearing and disappearing among tall weeds, and then struck by an idea, it urging me to go back and talk to the man who bought the jewelry. He must know someone who can help me I thought and informed the girls about returning to the city.

Wasting no time I headed out, taking the diamond necklace folded in a piece of cloth tied securely around my waist, just as she had done before.

As I turned eastward into the road, for a fleeting moment, I caught a sight of dog that was unmistakably Tenshi. He would have stealthily followed me to guard all the way to the city and back, if he had not been spotted. "Come here." I commanded, and Tenshi came whimpering, crawling on his belly, expecting to be punished for disobeying my order to stay at home and guard Miss Tami and Yumi in my absence. I squatted in front of the shivering Tenshi, gently lifted his jaw and looked into his eyes. *"You must return to your duty. I appreciate your concern for my safety, but the mission I am about to undertake has to be done without my worrying about Yumi and Miss Tami. We have very important responsibilities, but I will be comforted in knowing you are there to protect them. Now go back, I must be on my way."*

Tenshi understood, and he looked at me for a moment, and then turned and ran back in the direction of the farmhouse, disappearing quickly out of sight.

Trekking eastward, I covered the kilometers in good time, as passing the villages, noticing changes has been made since my previous trip. The former residents have returned, and women and children were working together to build a shack, salvaging the burnt but still useful pieces of wood from the piles of debris, their faces and hands blackened with smudges, while the men were doing the heavy work.

Those men were ex-Imperial Army soldiers, who had survived the war and returned home to their families for a happy reunion. But to an each returnee's dismay, the house he once lived in was burned to the ground and his wife and children's whereabouts were unknown; having nowhere to go or to stay, he had no choice but to live on the street.

Adding to his dismay, he did not receive his due compensation; the promised rewards for returnees upon his return home, but inevitably promised money were spent to support the war, and they were only allowed to keep the tattered fatigue he has warned to come home. Welcome-home gestures to honor their service to the Emperor were forsaken, and ex-soldier's downcast unsmiling eyes revealed his shattered spirit. Although some has found minimal work in exchange for a small meal, but for the most, without a choice, they became thieves, beggars, and sadly some of them has simply lost their minds, wandering in the street until illness and starvation terminated his life, ended his suffering.

Entering the Fukouka city limit, I heard the sound of unfamiliar music in the air, and the melodies were popular American songs to comfort the GIs, a long way from home. Heading north in the direction of the Iwataya, there were amazing changes, instead of tons of debris. The rows of small shopping stalls lining both sides of the street, and to my amazement, the rare sight of cosmetics, fabrics, many food items, tobacco, and liquors—anything one could wish for were sold, and attracting the herds of people, and they were buying goods even had the astronomical prices. But some of the people are looking and wondering, where did all these suddenly available fancy goods come from? As I have wondered.

During four years of war, all those goods were nonexistent;

one could only wonder how someone could have manufactured so many in such a short time. The only feasible explanation was, the merchants has defied the government's order to produce only war essentials, but they were manufacturing frivolous goods, prohibited by the government, to be sold at the black market.

Passing by the stalls, I searched for the man who bought my jewelry, drowning in the earsplitting loud music blaring from many of those shops. *"Mercy!?"* I cried out loud, but my voice was drowned out in the loud music and street noise, and then I saw a peculiar sight of a small Japanese girl wearing heavy make-up, fancy flimsy dress, and she was hanging onto an arm of a GI who was twice her height. The sight stabbed my heart.

The girl was a prostitute, a streetwalker, a product of the post-war, and those girls wore heavy make-up and bright-colored flimsy dresses to solicit sex, calling out,

"Hey, GI, camu my hausu, me giibu guudo taimu." speaking the only English words she knows. Ironically, hidden beneath the hideous make-up and cheap dress was a brave soul who sold her small frail body to support herself and her entire family. In the post-war era, there were no offices, shops, or restaurants to gain employment and had no other alternative, many girls—even those who were educated and came from upscale families. And to survive, she fell into a pit of misery.

That girl could have been me, Yumi, or heaven forbid, Miss Tami. I thought, doused with an ice-cold shiver, and an overwhelming urge to run away from there, but instead, I offered a prayer of sympathy for that girl, then turned and headed into the river of people.

I passed the cubicles, peering into the rows of each shop, hoping to find that man who bought my jewels. But eventually I was at a point of ready to give up my search, but then at an end of a row I saw him. He was sitting behind a large table full of his wares reading a newspaper.

"Good afternoon, sir," I called out to attract his attention. The man looked up and stared at me, who looked familiar to him, trying to jog his memory.

"Sir, again I came a long way to seek you out, and I am glad I've found you. It's been a while; I trust you're in good health?" I have greeted the man.

By the way, my name is Taka. I am a servant of the Araki family, and we have met before. I have introduced myself; it was time we knew each other by our proper names.

"Indeed—I remember now." The man said, having recognition in his eyes. *"My name is Mr. Ohara. Glad to make your acquaintance. So have you come to see me with another business deal?"*

"Yes, sir, I have an important mission that only your wisdom and knowledge will enable me to accomplish." I began.

"What that might be? By the way, you have a way with words; tell me what I can do for you."

"May I come inside, sir? It's awkward standing outside speaking to you across the display table, because the matters which I must confide are for your eyes and ears only," I have requested.

Chapter 8: Life Anew

Safely behind the enclosure, obscured from outside view, I removed the sash from my waist and exposed the diamond necklace, felt the weight of the flawless brilliant diamonds coiled in my palm, outshining one another with sparkling prisms as if it were alive. Emerged from behind the enclosure, holding the sash in my hand and walked up to Mr. Ohara handed him the folded clothe.

Mr. Ohara took the folded sash and concealed himself behind the curtain.

"Mmmm," I heard the sound of a groan; apparently Mr. Ohara was choked on his own breath, seeing the exquisite diamond necklace. A few moments passed, and Mr. Ohara stepped out from the enclosure. His eyes were wide open, and the astonished expression on his face show his feelings loudly.

Suppressing my jumpy nerves, I seized the moment to put on an air of authority.

"Sir, the price of this necklace is two million yen. Can you handle it?" I spoke with a deliberate bold tone of voice, trying to cover my shaky emotions.

"A-a-a-a—moment please, I-I need to think," Mr. Ohara said unable to conceal his vehement emotion, but as a businessman he needed a clear-thinking head regardless of the situation, and he tried to regain his composure. Two million yen, he thought. And an image of the brilliant diamonds' spellbinding fire was whirling in his head.

"Sir, your answer, please." I have prompted, and then to my surprise Mr. Ohara agreed with my price quote, also informing me he needed to contact a man named Mr. Aoki, his associate who fenced felonious merchandise. Mr. Aoki had many connections, so I must wait until a buyer would be found.

"If I may ask what would you do with that huge amount of money?" Mr. Ohara had to ask, out of his curiosity. I thought for a moment, and then told him about the impending project of building a house.

"I see. Mr. Aoki will be just the right man to be your service." And Mr. Ohara also told me that this might take some time, so I should stay at an inn until the buyer could be found.

I chose an inn close to the market area, but the place turned out to be a flophouse frequented by prostitutes.

"No matter—all I need is a place to sleep for one or two nights." But that was a mistaken assumption, as my stay stretched to a week. Throughout the duration of her stay, there were sounds of constant coming and going day and night, loathsome, trashy music was played loudly, and nauseating erotic noises coming through the paper-thin walls; sometimes I felt movements from the next room, transmitted through the floor and the wall, but I had to stay put until the diamond necklace has to be sold.

Mr. Aoki was a frequent customer at Mr. Ohara's infamous establishment, but during the war the prostitution house was burned to the ground, and Mr. Ohara has lost contact with Mr.

Aoki however, coincidently the two men has ran into an each other at the black market, and they rejoiced the reunion, and then one thing led to another, partnership was born and their friendship was renewed, and they were the perfect partners in fencing. Mr. Aoki has used his position, discreetly buying and selling merchandise through underground connections. They kept other fences from gaining the profitable information involving their extraordinary merchandise.

Mr. Aoki was employee of the Air Force, and he was a construction foreman, had a special U.S. truck driver's license, which enabled him to pass through the guarded gate, merely showing his license. Thus, able him to pass through without any fear of being stopped and searched; he would only smile and wave his hand to the MP, who knows him by a sight. Mr. Aoki took an advantage of having the US driver's license; he has carried away many U.S. goods, concealed under the bulk of wood and refuses to be incinerated. But he delivered these goods straight to black market where the customers were waiting, and they have immediately bought all he had. Also the imperfect lumber was discarded for a reason of having warped or knots, cannot be used in construction, but many of the pieces were in perfectly good condition, as far as the frugal know-how Japanese were concerned, and their ingenuity made it work even to build houses.

Aside from the discarded lumber, Mr. Aoki used his clout as a foreman to get his hands on a variety of the American merchandises which sold at the PX and commissary, and the merchandise were to be sold only to the GIs and the officers' families. Mr. Aoki sold the U.S. products, such as sugar, cigarettes, clothing, coffee ground (which used once and dried was sold in the street for forty-five US dollars a pound), and many more goods, Japanese could not obtain because those goods were none existent.

In the meantime, exact replicas of counterfeit U.S. goods were flooding the market, even had the Made in America seal and indistinguishable to the Japanese who could not read English; the contents, however, were unfit for consumption. So when people saw a fence in the marketplace, which validated the authenticity of his merchandise, everything he brought was sold as fast as grown wings, no matter the high prices.

The base employees were searched at the gate, upon leaving from work, however, if the confiscated goods were found on them, even a pack of chewing gum, which has warranted an instant dismissal.

Mr. Ohara informed Mr. Aoki about the house to be built, and told him that the buyer would need as many truckloads of lumber as he could get. Hmmm, truckloads? Mr. Aoki thought, and he was overwhelmed by the enormity of his responsibility, but after a quick calculation, he would gain enormous profits and being paid in cash has made his defining decision.

Mr. Aoki agreed to take the job, along with the responsibility of finding strong able-bodied workmen, which was not a problem, because there were homeless ex-Imperial soldiers who would jump at a chance to have food and shelter, as a payment for gainful employment.

Mr. Aoki has set out to find a fence he could trust, to avoid the leak of a huge business transaction to another fences, which were looking eagerly for a chance to make money. He needed the tools, but those had to be acquired discreetly to avoid suspicion when dealing with the fellow fences. Although the lumber pieces were discarded items, but if he was caught selling them, Mr. Aoki would be arrested for grand theft. These thoughts kept him in a dither; and his mind was running in circles.

Every day I made a trip to Mr. Ohara's shop, hoping for

information about a buyer, but his answer was always the same as the day before, *"Not yet. Check with me tomorrow."* Mr Ohara said, and I was beginning to doubt that the Mr. Aoki's promise to find a buyer.

Then on the sixth day, the moment I walked in, *"We have a buyer!"* Mr. Ohara said emphatically nodding his head, also that the Mr. Aoki came by a night before to inform him about the lumber and a buyer for the gems.

According to Mr. Aoki, recruiting the workers was no problem, because there were many who would work for food and shelter. As for a buyer for the diamond necklace, Mr. Aoki had a possible candidate on standby.

"How soon will I meet this man?" I asked, my voice raising a notch higher. The meeting was to take place that morning, and an American officer and his interpreter would be there before noon. I felt an exhilarating expectation about the sale; suddenly the whole world seemed much brighter. I hurried back to the Inn to make myself presentable.

Prior to leaving the inn, I have calmly sat down, closed my eyes to block out all the external stimuli, and prayed for the Buddha's grace to be my guidance.

A very tall middle-aged American officer arrived at Mr. Ohara's shop, with his interpreter, and I was informed of the officer asked to see the diamond necklace immediately. It was the first time I have stood so close to an American, which caused me to become overwhelmingly anxious, not knowing how to greet the officer or say something appropriate, nervously I unfolded the cloth and exposed the diamond necklace.

The officer took one look at the brilliant diamonds and inhaled a big breath, eyes glued on the rows of diamonds shooting a sparkling prism, and then he exhaled slowly. Turning to his interpreter, and the officer said something to him, while the interpreter nodded after each word the officer spoke.

"*The officer has agreed and pays the amount of twenty-five thousand dollars, approximately three million yen.*" The interpreter relayed. However, the officer was aware that this necklace was an antique, museum-quality piece; judging by the gold clasp and the cut of those diamonds, the true value had to be much more than Taka's asking price. The officer had never saw before a brilliant piece of gem, he felt in his heart he has found extraordinary one of its kind jewelry, and he believed price of this jewelry was much more than twenty-five thousand dollars.

"*I must make the money transaction from Stateside, and I will return as soon as I can.*" The interpreter relayed the officer's words, and I thought about the three million yen, an unheard sum of money—more than the Japanese government had in the treasury vault. Repeating to myself, the necklace was sold, I was ecstatic, and more I thought about it the truth of sale became more real to me, and three days later the necklace and the money has exchanged ownership.

I thanked Mr. Ohara for the entire transaction, and informing him I will return with the plans to build the house in few days, and I gave two thousand yen to Mr. Ohara as a gratuity and immediately departing thereafter. I headed back home ecstatically elated; my quickened paces barely left footprints on the road, as if I was walking on a cloud.

Passing through the villages, I have noticed there were more refugees returning to build shacks to reclaim their lives, and some of them even had small patches of vegetable gardens and already sprouting tiny green leaves, a welcome sign of hope. Feeling a jubilant surge of happy future would be waiting for them from this day forward, and we would begin our life anew without any fear of the war.

Turning into the path to the farmhouse there sat Tenshi, and he sprung to his feet running to greet his master, wagging his tail as if it would flies off, I hugged Tenshi whimpered with joy, and then we raced home.

After six long days of separation, we were joyously reunited, and I could not stop talking about my experiences in the big city, how the extreme change has created a foreign milieu, thus the country's proud superiority was erased, Tami and Yumi could not imagine what their future would entail; believing Japan was no longer their own country.

Again the government propaganda was at work, convincing the citizens to hate the evil Americans, for they will make all of us their slaves; it was a last ditch effort to save face of the government. However, those GIs I saw in the city and the officer I have met were far from the government portrayal of an evil they projected, but Tami and Yumi were still very fearful.

"Come with me to the city," I urged. *"The Americans are not evil; see them for yourselves."*

Reluctantly they agreed, and the three of us headed out to the city, towing the cart to bring back supplies, but Tenshi stayed behind to guard the farmhouse. Coming close to the city limit, I stopped to ask people, *"Is there a quiet Inn nearby?"* Luckily there was one not far away, but the Inn has not been opened for some time because the owner would not allow prostitutes to practice their quick turnover business. We followed a narrow dirt road as directed, but the surrounding wooded landscape did not give any sign of an Inn ahead. Having no choice we kept going ahead, praying they had not been misled us. The day was ending and the evening afterglow has begun to fade.

"Taka, where are we? It's getting so dark I can't see the road ahead of us anymore," Miss Tami said fearfully.

"According to the direction I received, we should be there at any moment," I answered. Acting cheerful, but I was just as uncertain as desperately asking Buddha to lead us to the Inn.

At that moment Yumi yelled,

"Look I see a light!" She pointed her finger to the flickering dim light in between the trees.

"At last! Let us hurry before they lock the door." I said began to run, pulling the cart along the narrow path. Tami held on to the shaking and bumping cart, until we were at front of an the Inn, which had tall poll with a round glass ball atop dimly lit by small light bulb, illuminating letters INN, although most of it has washed off by the passing years. Encouraged by the sign, I knocked on the door, but no one answered so I knocked harder, and then a dim light came on inside, followed by the sound of approaching quickened footsteps.

"Just a moment, I'm coming." a woman's voice said, and the door slid open just enough to peer through.

"We're in need of a night's lodging. Can you accommodate us?" I inquired.

The woman became relaxed to find her guests were young females, and she knew from her years of experience they were not prostitutes. Welcoming them, she lent her hand to pull the cart inside the gates for safekeeping, and carrying their belongings ushered them through a dark hallway into a small, dimly lit room.

I realized, during the war, there were no bright light bulbs; only a twenty-five-watt bulb was available, even now.

"Begging your pardon, ma'am, we were unprepared for arriving guests—it has been almost a year since anyone has stopped by—but

please do not be concerned. My mother is an excellent cook, and she will be happy to make a meal to satisfy your palates. Please make yourselves comfortable. I will immediately prepare the bath for you, and I will return shortly with your hot meal. Thank you for your patronage." The woman expressed her gratitude, bowed and exited quietly, closing the shoji sliding door.

Before long she returned to let them know the bath was ready. Tami was the first to bathe. The bathtub was an old-fashioned deep cast-iron bowl situated outside, and the water was heated by burning wood under it; a wooden disk floated on top. Bathing outdoors was not a problem, since they were used to bathing in the hot spring pond.

Tami washed her body outside of the tub and carefully pushed the wooden disk to the bottom with her foot, and then got herself into the tub, trying not to touch the sides of the hot tub with her body.

Refreshed and glowing with the warmth of a hot bath, Tami returned to the room, and greeted with the aroma of delicious miso soup. There was an individual tray of food, and bowl of miso soup that had goodly portion of cubed tofu, the season's vegetables, and a raw egg being cooked dropped in the steaming broth.

"Soup's on, ma'am." the woman announced cheerfully, placing a tray in front of each of us. A large bowl of steamed rice, sliced yellow pickled radish, and fragrant hot green tea was a meal fit for the Emperor, and we consumed it with gusto. Full and comfortable, the girls fell fast asleep on the soft futon mattresses with pillows under their heads.

An early morning luminescence filtered through the shoji door into the room, and clattering sounds from the kitchen had waken me, but for a moment I did not know where I was and glanced over to find Tami and Yumi still sound asleep. We have arrived late last night totally fatigued, but soon the tantalizing aroma of a morning meal had wakened Tami and Yumi out of their sound sleep.

"Good morning, ma'am. May I come in? I brought hot tea for you." the woman greeted, speaking from behind the closed shoji door, and upon entering, she said, *"I hope you had good night sleep, ma'am, this here green tea is the best we have, only for our guests, and I will bring the morning meal shortly. If I may, it is a pleasure to serve our guests. My name is Naomi and my mother and I will do our best to make your stay comfortable."* Naomi was an attractive middle-aged woman, looking younger than her age.

"We're fortunate to have found your establishment last night. This is our Miss Tami, the only survivor of the Araki family, and I am Taka and this is Yumi, my sister. We are Miss Tami's servants and bodyguards. Also we have a German shepherd named Tenshi who guards us all, but he stayed behind to guard our home."

"We may stay for a few days to take care of our business. Perhaps you know of someone who will taxi us into the town?" I inquired.

"Yes, I know a rickshaw man who used to provide the taxi service; he has serviced my guests when people were traveling during peacetime. He used to station himself in front of my Inn; ready to be of service, but since my Inn has been a vacant for so long he has not worked for almost a year. But I know where he lives, so I will go and fetch him. I'm sure he will be happy to be of service." Naomi said, her eyes sparkling with gratitude of serving guests.

"I appreciate your effort, and here are two thousand yen for an advance payment." I said, handed the money to Naomi, and she accepted with both of her hands bowed deeply, as if she was offering a prayer.

"Thank you, ma'am." Naomi thanked us, and she thought, it

has been a year since my mother and I had any income; I know we're going to be all right; we will survive.

As the girls were relaxing after consuming Mama-san's soul-warming meal, Naomi returned to inform them the rickshaw man would be arriving shortly.

A lean old man wearing the traditional navy blue happy coat, matching shorts and a Japanese flag bandana securely tied around his head, exercising his legs readying himself for the long run ahead. His lean brown body was permanently tanned from years of running as a rickshaw man. When we came out, he bowed humbly and ushered us up into his clean and polished black rickshaw.

But the three of them sitting in the small cab was a tight fit; the rickshaw man smiled broadly to ensure all would be well, and as he smiled his eyes disappeared in between the wrinkles, exposing his gleaming white teeth from ear to ear. We acknowledged with nods and smiles, we were on way. He ran smoothly without bumping or shaking, the skill rickshaw man has perfected for his customers.

Upon arriving in downtown Fukuoka, I handed five hundred yen to the rickshaw man and told him to wait until ready to return. Overwhelmed to receive so much money for his service, he removed his bandana in respect and bowed many times to show his thanks.

Tami and Yumi were awed to see the changes that had taken over the city, and noticing many fancily dressed women browsing through the shops, but we were embarrassed to be seen wearing the oversized gardeners' garb and large black pig-toed rubber booties. Quickly, I have led them into a small eatery to avoid being stared at, and then I headed over to Mr. Ohara's to make arrangements to meet with Mr. Aoki.

After returning to the eatery, I have made suggestion to find and purchase some presentable attire, stepped out into the stream of people, walked toward the shopping stalls, hoping to find dresses, perhaps blouses and skirts, and the pairs of shoes. After searching through all those shops, however, we could not find any item that we were looking for, but at a pawnshop Tami found a sophisticated pale gray suit and a pair of black pumps exactly her size, and judging from the condition of the suit, those must have been a treasured possession of some young lady. In addition, and I bought some soft blankets someone had given up for a small sum, and more of ensembles, but shoes were difficult to find, so I bought a few pairs of flimsy zori (flip-flops) until I find shoes. I barrowed Tami's suite and shoes to keep an appointment with Mr. Aoki, and before long a middle aged man of average height and weight, which was small in comparison to the Americans, appeared in front of the shop.

"Mr. Aoki, you're very punctual. Taka herself arrived shortly before you." Mr. Ohara said, introduced me to Mr. Aoki, and he made a suggestion to conduct our meeting in a more private location, instead of having to contend with the constant stream of onlookers. And Mr. Aoki chose a small teahouse about ten minutes walk away from Mr. Ohara's shop.

According to Mr. Aoki, recruiting laborers was not a problem, because many homeless ex-Imperial soldiers would jump at a chance to work for food. The every piece of lumber was stamped GRADE A, sent from the United Sates to build housing and for various construction needs, but during an inspection Mr. Aoki discovered some of the lumber had many knots, cracks, or even warped, and these pieces were discarded by the truckload. But as far as the Japanese were concerned, all those discards were in perfectly good condition, and the frugal-minded genius Japanese builders knew exactly how to get around those flaws and make the material work.

Having cleared the first hurdle, I have requested the construction begin as soon as possible, and I asked Mr. Aoki to be the construction foreman; also as a reward, I added the bonuses for him and his men, for building house to be done as soon as possible, and Mr. Aoki agreed and the business meeting was successfully concluded.

In the meantime, care packages were sent from the U.S. Red Cross, containing gifts of much-needed foods, medical supplies, and clothing, which were donated by the generous American citizens and distributed to the destitute Japanese people. However, many of these foods were foreign to the Orientals, but the grateful Japanese has managed and as a result, starvation was no longer a problem.

Furthermore, the U.S. Army Corps of Engineers has restored damaged railways; employing Japanese manpower and they paved the dirt roads full of potholes even a jeep could not pass. Also for the first time, the new paved roads had actual wide sidewalks, replacing a painted line, a foot and a half wide, indicating a walking space. No longer would the grateful Japanese pedestrians have a fear of being pushed nor have to jump away from bicycles zipping past. The commuter train service was also restored, enabling the citizens to enjoy life's amenities with gratitude. The American has selflessly shared all this with the Japanese people, who never knew such a pleasure of life until now.

Prompted by the caring Americans' gestures, the Japanese government has released foods and commodities, which were reserved only for the Imperial hierarchy, but to be distributed to the public by rationing monthly and this was an extra bonus people have not expected, although the allotted food lasted only a few days.

After concluding the business dealing with Mr. Aoki, we were ready to return to the village, but after having to indulge ourselves with the comfort of sleeping on a soft futon, and luxuries of having our needs met at every turn were hard to forego.

"Taka, I wish to remain here." Miss Tami said wistfully, she was caught in the dilemma of being unwilling to return to resume a near-primitive existence. I understood—in fact all three of us has shared the sentiment—but I had an appointment to keep without fail with Mr. Aoki, so I must return to the village, and I have made an arrangement with Naomi, for us to stay on indefinitely and departed alone.

Every day Tenshi has been waiting for me at a turnoff to farmhouse, and he caught the sight of me, came dashing ecstatically happy to have me back home, but he kept looking for Tami and Yumi. Squatting in front of Tenshi, I whispered to him that the girls were in the city where they are safe and protected. Although there was an apprehension in Tenshi eyes, but he understood.

When I have returned from the city, looks as if the farmhouse has further dilapidated; but standing with its remaining strength to welcome me home, and Tenshi and I have shared food, staying close together in the darkened house, and before long, fatigue has lured me into a deep sleep, while Tenshi kept his visual over me.

The next morning I waited for Mr. Aoki, at the estate's entrance gates, when nearing noon an army truck arrived carrying the cargo of lumber and five workmen. They soon discovered the carriage driveway was too narrow for the army truck to pass through, not only too narrow, but also massive overgrown weeds prevented access to the estate. Immediately, the men began to clear the path by cutting and pulling all the growth. Finally they walked up to the estate, and they faced with more of the massive growth. Realizing the enormity of their task, they set to clearing more bushes and piles of debris.

While the men were unloading the lumber, and carrying it up to the cleared spot, Mr. Aoki was assessing the situation and returned to the city for more building supplies.

The following day, Mr. Aoki and the workmen were back at dawn and began to clear away the debris, saving it for firewood. Rebuilding the cooking grill was at the top of their agenda; it would be constructed over the same place where the kitchen once was, also they have repaired the well pump, which provided plenty of cool drinking water. A bucket of water was suspended from a beam overhead for a shower, and a crude shack had to be built for them to bed down at night.

Mr. Aoki has negotiated with fellow fences many more times, for more needed items, and an each time upon his returning to the estate he found that work has progressed, and the preparations was in progress to build Tami's house, where the Mistress Shizuka's living quarters once stood. Shinto priest was summoned to perform a traditional blessing of the land, facing east first where the sun rises, south to north, and to the west in a circle of four points, reciting the prayer and performing an exorcism to ward off evil spirits before the work began, insuring the safe progress and completion of the happy home.

Chapter 9: Celebration

When Miss Tami was still an infant, her grandfather has built a child-size teahouse, and he hosted the traditional rice-cake-throwing ceremony, using small mochi, a round rice cake made from steamed mashed rice, in honor of the firstborn granddaughter, but today in the current postwar crisis, Tami knew many people were still suffering, so she decided to celebrate the occasion by sharing a simple meal with her immediate family under the skeletal structure of her house.

The news was welcomed, and wasting no time the men began constructing a deck for a large dining area, to be a floor of house, and a large table to accommodate ten people. Two men volunteered to gather clams on the day of the celebration. Tami had invited Mr. Ohara and Mr. Aoki as their guests of honor, so to inform them, I rode the recently restored fast and comfortable train to the city, went straight to Mr. Ohara's establishment, and presented him with Miss Tami's invitation for the upcoming celebration, as her guests of honor.

And I have conferred with Mr. Ohara about obtaining

contraband food and sake, hearing my request, immediately he sent a message out to few of his chosen fences, and in no time all those goods were delivered to Mr. Ohara's shop, and concealed under the display table, draped over with a tablecloth. Although the goods were not in public view, but those had to be remove promptly from his premises to avoid being discovered.

At dusk, I have summoned a rickshaw, quickly loaded the contrabands, with the help of Mr. Ohara and the rickshaw man, and vacated the premises before anyone would notice. Then I was faced with transporting all those goods to the village without being caught in the MP's inspection raids, which were periodically conducted. Returning to the village on foot was out of question; not only was the risk of being robbed, but also the journey would take two days. After thinking it through, I have decided to chance a journey by the train; that would be the simplest and fastest way, and take only an hour and a half.

An early the next morning, I tied the sack of rice to my abdomen, and wore Mama-san's old kimono to disguise myself as a pregnant housewife, arrived at the train station, but to her surprise no one paid any attention to me, and as luck would have it, there were no MPs in sight. The train was full of passengers who bought foods from the expensive black market, and they carried parcels of contraband large and small without any concealment, taking a chance of being caught in a raid just as I have.

Swiftly the train ran westbound, and monotonous scenery sped past the windows, while the fast-turning metal wheels beat out the loud repetitious rhythm. No one spoke, some had fallen asleep, and their weary grim expressions have conveyed the heavy responsibilities of they have to go an extreme to purchase necessary staples, only black market has, to feed their family were clearly shown on face even as they slept.

The train came to its final stop, and all the passengers disembarked carrying the heavy parcels on their backs and in their hands. My back ached from carrying the ten-kilo, (approximately twelve pound) sack of rice tied to my abdomen, and a parcel in each hand, walking was arduous, I have stopped many times to rest before reaching the estate; for the next trip I will take a workman poses as my husband to assist transporting the goods.

At dawn on the celebration day, two workmen headed down to the seashore carrying a crude bamboo fishing pole equipped with a hook made of a bent nail and a bucket to carry their catch. The table was placed on the deck waiting for the arrival of Tami, Yumi, and the invited guests, while men and I were busily preparing the food to be cooked. They all hoped the guests of honor would arrive without encountering any problems, because they were bringing more contraband items.

The two fishermen returned about noon with a huge flounder. The pole was skewered through the fish's gills, and with the pole ends resting on their shoulders the men managed to carry the bucket full of clams, oysters, and large crabs. *"Ooh, wonderful! This fish is so big it'll feed all of us, and those oysters and clams—we'll have a grand feast,"* I exclaimed. The cooking pit was fired up, and in no time an appetizing aroma of steaming rice and grilling flounder began drifting in the air.

Tenshi was sitting a few feet away, watching me grilled fish, waiting patiently to get a piece of morsel, and every scrap I tossed in his direction, he caught in a midair never missed a piece.

In the ominous postwar era, in a small corner of the world, under an umbrella of warm sunshine, and few puffs of white clouds drifting in the blue sky, a group of fortunate people were celebrating having the foods and beverages others could only dream of.

Tami and Yumi arrived, but Mr. Aoki and Mr. Ohara had not, and time was passing without any sign of their invited guests. Everything was ready, and I could no longer keep the food hot without ruining them, so the feast began, and everything was consumed with gusto.

An evening afterglow has enflamed the sky with orange fire, but soon faded away to soft pink, and then gray dusk swallowed remaining faint light. The men sipped hot sake and leisurely engaged in small talk, a simple treasured moment of sharing a camaraderie which was lost in times past until tonight.

"I wish Mr. Ohara and Mr. Aoki were here to enjoy all these wonderful foods. I know they would've enjoyed it," one man wondered out loud.

"I hope nothing has happened to them," another commented, and they knew about MP's raid.

I was genuinely concerned about them, looking up at the darkening sky.

"I pray the two men did not run into a raid, having contraband in their possession." I have voiced my concern. But the penalties for being caught with the contrabands in their position were heavy find and the incarceration. Also I had an immediate problem of where Tami and Yumi would sleep tonight, too late for the last run.

"Dear me, I have completely forgotten about the time. Judging from the darkness it's too late for the last train. I beg your pardon, ma'am," I apologized to Miss Tami and Yumi.

Hearing that comment, the men offered their shelter for the girls, and they would sleep on the deck under the stars, commenting it was their way of life not too long ago even in a cold rainy night.

Suddenly, Mr. Ohara and Mr. Aoki emerged out of the

darkness, carrying a huge parcel slung over their shoulder. *"My word! Mr. Ohara, Mr. Aoki, we had given up on you."* I exclaimed, and everyone greeted the two men with joy, glad to see the two men.

"Please, tell us what happened? We were so worried." I asked, relieved to see very hungry two men.

"We started out to the Iwataya train station to catch the six a.m. The first run," Mr. Aoki began, and Mr. Ohara nodded to confirm, and all of us were listening while the two men unfold their predicament, I have prepared the foods as quickly as I could, knowing how hungry they must be.

When we approached the train station, there were a few jeeps with the MP logo parked in front, and we watched the entrance to the train station from a building across the street, and just as we thought, the MPs and the Japanese police were conducting a raid, inspecting all the passengers' parcels, looking for black market contraband. Mr. Aoki paused and inhaled deeply to collect his thoughts.

"We knew about the surprise raids and deployed at any given time, but we took a chance hoping they would not have raid today. You know if you are caught with contraband all the goods will be confiscated and a high penalty will be imposed. The situation was alarming. If we got caught having all those U.S.–issued goods, I would be fired and sent to the brig, and my partner here would be arrested by the Japanese police." Mr. Aoki said, glancing at Mr. Ohara.

I knew about those worn items to be incinerated, for hygiene reasons and the strict regulation was enforced, but I had confiscated the less-worn pieces, like towels, sheets, and blankets were laundered at the base laundry, and we brought them as house-warming gifts, because most of them were almost new, not a worn spot on them.

"We picked up our bags and left stealthily, and anxiously waited for the next departure time, and then picked up our bags again and went back to the train station, but the MP jeeps were still parked in the same spot." Mr. Aoki said.

"What d'ya think? Maybe we ought to give it up?" Mr. Aoki has commented, realizing situation was hopeless. But Mr. Ohara was adamant not to give up.

"Think of all our friends be waiting for us, we couldn't quit now, imagine how disappointed and worried they would be, thinking something bad have happened to us."

"No…We couldn't give up now." Mr. Ohara shouted at me.

The darkness began to consume daylight, while our arduous task of going to and from the train station continued. But each time we made our way there, those jeeps have not moved, as if grown roots. By now the departure time for the last train was fast approaching, so for the final time, we headed out to the station.

And then there in front of the Iwataya train station, empty parking spaces loomed like a child's lost front teeth. The jeeps were gone, which meant the MPs and Japanese police were gone." The coast was clear.

"We hauled the bags up on our shoulders and ran through hordes of people, all carrying as many bags as they could." Mr. Aoki was visualizing the mobs of people scurrying desperately to get on the last run train, all wanting to get home.

"They were hiding from the MPs, just as we were," Mr. Ohara stated.

We ran to head off the rushing mob of mostly females, forcing and pushing past them with our male strength, and got ourselves into a train that was already packed tight past its capacity, just in time for the conductor to close the door. We all squeezed against each other, and then he blew a whistle signaling the train's departure. The train jerked hard with a bang, jerked two more times and began to move slowly gaining speed, moving faster and faster, leaving many people standing on the darkening platform.

"Sure felt sorry for those women." Mr. Ohara said remorsefully, visualizing all those grim faces quickly drowned by the night's darkness.

After Mr. Aoki and Mr. Ohara told their story, the girls retired to the shack, the workmen had generously given up for the night. Although Miss Tami couldn't go back to the comfortable Inn tonight, at least she would have a roof over her head.

Submersed in a veil of balmy night air, the men sat in a circle of light, as ribbons of amber flame waved upwards as if reaching into a night sky splashed with the stars hanging high and low, as though one could touch them. Dark shadows of clouds passed every so often, disappearing beyond the horizon to the dawning morning on the other side of the earth. Cascading silvery beams showered down from the reigning moon and veiled the landscape, transforming it into a haunting abstract phenomenon of eerie black and silver.

The forgotten ex-Imperial soldiers, for the first time, bonded in brotherhood, they shared the memories of bygone years deeply tucked away in his soul. The ribbons of flames had died down, and amber charcoal would soon be gone, leaving only warmth under the ashes.

Pitching a tent over the platform with the army blankets Mr. Aoki brought, and men fell into a blissful sleep, feeling warm glow of sake, wrapped in blanket of the camaraderie. The girls bedded down lying under the blankets Mr. Aoki had unscrupulously acquired, as housewarming gifts, which proved more valuable than he realized.

The house begun to take its shape and two workmen have been

meticulously cleaning the riverbed, picking off every bit of debris, and washing smudged blackened pebbles, until sparkling white. The flagstones were lifted up from the walkway and scrubbed clean, looked as if stone had been polished. Servants dug up some hibiscuses from the village and transplanted to complement the garden.

Yumi and I have been working tirelessly to make the house as comfortable as possible, using the sheets and blankets to cover the walls and floor. At last all was finished, ready for Miss Tami to take the possession of her house.

The day has arrived for Miss Tami to move in, and Yumi, Tenshi, and Workmen were lined up to welcome their mistress to her new home. Before Miss Tami entered, she stopped for a moment, to see an image of her smiling mother, grandfather, and her father, realizing they were always at her side, assuring her the worst of the war was over, and her future would not be threatened again.

The house faced south just as her mother's quarters had, and offered her comfort and sanctuary with a view of an infinite horizon, the grand view remaining just as it had been for thousands of years.

"Miss Tami, your evening meal will be served directly, and the bath's ready for you, ma'am." Yumi announced, as she has in the past when the world was at peace, and all was well.

The first day of the Miss Tami's homecoming was getting closer; she hoped this was the first step in reestablishing her former way of life. But life in Japan would never be the same again, and the tidal wave of postwar era has drowned traditional Japanese culture and threw the country into upheaval. The backbone of family tradition and simple peaceful lifestyle known to the world over has been trampled to death. The people had fallen into a cauldron of vicious survival-of-the-fittest, only thing that has remained unchanged was the sun rising in the morning and setting in the evening.

Influenced by contemporary eastern culture, defiant younger generation has revolted against the centuries-old tradition of feudalism, brandishing their egotistic attitudes of down with the establishment! And to make their statement wore tie-dyed T-shirts and threadbare blue jeans, deliberately unkempt, copying the hippies' mantra to throw a mockery at the government and establishments, proclaiming, "Nothing's real; do your own thing." Sadly, not so long ago, these defiant young men were law-abiding proper young citizens, who had been brought up to respect the elders, parents, and laws of the country.

Mr. Aoki visited the estate frequently, and he brought gifts of rare items such as perfumed bath soap, Max Factor cosmetics, toothbrushes, and toothpaste, etc… also he often brought a jug of sake for his soul brothers, and as always his visits ended with a feast, even though sharing only steamed rice and a bowl of miso soup.

One day, Miss Tami was looking out the window wistfully, remembering as a small child, seeing the beautifully restored garden through her misty eyes, seeing herself strolling the garden just like this with her grandfather, holding onto his hand before the fire destroyed everything.

I came in and interrupted Miss Tami with an important request, in behalf of a workman representing the others.

"What is your wish?" Miss Tami asked, pulling herself away from her long-ago memory of nostalgia.

"Begging your pardon, ma'am, we … Ahh … we wish to let you know how-how grateful we are to-to be working for you," he stammered.

"If I may, Miss Tami," I cut in. *"This here is Yoshiki, who had previously confided in me with an out-of-the-ordinary request, feared of your refusal,"* I stated.

"My name is Yoshiki Yanagawa, ma'am." Humbly he has introduced himself.

"So, Yoshiki, what is your wish? By the way, Taka, I don't know any of the men's names?" Miss Tami mentioned.

"I will make formal introductions after our talk." I said, and began to relay the men's requests.

At the time Mr. Aoki needed strong men to build a house, he knew there were many starving ex-Imperial Army soldiers roaming in the streets, and they would jump at a chance to work for food and shelter. But their chance of finding gainful job was next to none. Having no choice, they lived in the street and begged for handouts; unable to remember when was the last time they had anything to eat. And when Mr. Aoki came along to hire some of them, they fought off each other and eagerly offered themselves for an exchange of food and shelter, and Mr. Aoki chose five men.

"As you can see their promises were kept faithfully, and the work is nearing to an end. Meaning the reality of them becoming miserable homeless is getting closer with each passing day, and men would choose death rather than live on the street again. Working for you has regained pride as men who have purpose in his life, they wish to stay on as your servants, requiring no payment, only food and shelter," I concluded.

"I see." Miss Tami acknowledged the seriousness of the men's situation, and asked me to summon the other four men, who were waiting anxiously just outside of the front door, and as they entered, I have instructed them to introduce themselves to Miss Tami.

A man named Taro introduced himself first, and he began to tell Miss Tami of his life before the war. Taro Yoshida owned a small family catering business, and he and his wife produced ready-to-eat foods, which were artfully packaged in containers with their own logo and sold as box lunches. In addition, he catered for small parties on the side, but the war came and took him away. When he returned four years later, Taro was left with a heap of debris where his thriving business had been, and his wife was killed in a fire. Thus he was faced with the reality of being alone.

Next was Ken Kashiwahara, a single man, very handsome and strong, who could do any chore assigned for him. Although he never revealed his prior life, he was a pleasant and sociable man.

The third man was Hiroshi Saito, an ex-kamikaze pilot. He was the youngest and a former college student. Luckily the ending of the war spared his life, but he too found himself alone in front of a pile of charred debris, what was left of his family home. He was unable to find his family's whereabouts or even if they were dead or alive. Hiroshi had erected a crude shelter for himself, using charred wood that had been part of his family's home. The shelter had just enough space for him to crawl inside and have some protection from the outside elements, but leaked mercilessly when rained.

Yoshiki Yanagawa, another single man, was living with his family when he was drafted, but when he returned from the war he too found his entire neighborhood had been destroyed and exploding bombs has dug up the roads. He was unable to find his house or his family and desperately hungry, turned thief and stole food, when he could not find anything to steal.

The last of the five was a small man, and he was not a returnee, but he has climbed up on the truck, grabbing onto the side, and would not get off. He was small enough to pick up just as you would a child, but he wrapped his arms around a post of the truck, making an odd sound as if begging for a mercy. Mr. Aoki did not have the heart to kick him off, so this little man became a member of the work crew, and to their surprise, they discovered he was not only a mute, but deaf as well.

The little man could not tell his name, so they called him Ohi, meaning *"Hey you."* Although it sounded rude but no disrespect was intended, and Ohi knew it; he was always smiling showing a mouth full of teeth. Wasting no time, Ohi tilled some ground by an edge of the estate and planted sweet potatoes, which he had propagated from discarded peels. He also found edible wild vegetables and dug up taro roots in a ditch, transplanted them into his vegetable garden. Ohi even surprised everyone with an exquisite bonsai he created with a Japanese flowering plum tree. Ohi and Tenshi was inseparable, since both of them liked to scout around in the fields and ditches; while Ohi searched for edible plants, wild berries, and kept his eyes appealed for some suitable small tree to create a bonsai, Tenshi as always ran off after his prey.

After the introductions were over, Miss Tami agreed to the men's request without a second thought, and she told all five of them to stay as long as they wished, and for their future welfare, she would provide generous amenities for each of them; she also has made a mental note to put it in writing. Overwhelmed with gratitude, the five men swore to be her faithful servants, bowing deeply to show their respect.

With each passing day the estate bore greater resemblance to its former being. Yoshiki and Ohi spent hours on their hands and knees meticulously cleaning the riverbed, but Miss Tami grew restless watching the same goings-on every day. One day she has informed me wished to go to the city and to be escorted, so I thought it would do us good to have a change of scenery. And have a visit with Mr. Ohara and ask him to sell another piece of jewelry, Miss Tami and I boarded the express train headed for Fukuoka.

Precisely on schedule, the train came into the familiar Iwataya train station and halted smoothly without any jerking motion. Walking out to the boulevard, immediately we were swallowed into an ocean of walking people, and we were pushed about tried to make headway without being separated. A half of the boulevard had been claimed as a right of way for the American military vehicles, privately owned dependants' cars, and officers' limousines, thus not only people but also be on guard for bicycle riders zipping past left and right.

Finally, we came to the rows of small shops lining the street and headed for Mr. Ohara's shop. However, we found a stranger was occupying his shop. *"Excuse me, where's Mr. Ohara?"* I asked, being confused and frazzled.

"He moved to his new shop by the railway station." a wrinkled old woman answered from inside, and "Many pickpockets—be on guard all the time," she warned.

"Thank you kindly." I said, and we went back into the mob of pedestrians, remembering words of an old woman about the pickpockets, even more acutely aware of the gem-filled sash I had wrapped around my waist.

The railway station where Tenshi and I have found each other was about a mile to the south. The area surrounding the station has been changed drastically; and many more small shop stalls lined each side of the street in front of the station. We walked along peering into each stall, hoping to find Mr. Ohara, praying the old woman's information was correct. Finally there he was sitting inside of a much larger shop.

"Come in—come in, ladies. It's been a while. What brings you two here?" Mr. Ohara asked elatedly, surprised and happy to see us.

After exchanging the greetings, I have relayed the progress of estate and informed him about the diamond necklace to be sold.

Mr. Ohara asked us to come back the next day; that would give him time to contact Mr. Aoki.

After leaving Mr. Ohara's shop, I hailed a taxi and Miss Tami and I have headed for the Inn for a hot bath and Mama-san's home-cooked meals.

"We've missed you so much; it's been very lonely without you ladies. We're glad to have you back, even if it's only for a night," Naomi said jubilantly, and shortly she returned with a tray of fragrant hot green tea and sweet cakes; also she brought a newspaper. I looked over the newspaper, which did not have much of news articles, but savoring the fragrant tea and sweet cakes made up for the newspaper's lack of integrity. And then I noticed a want ad, in particular was written in Japanese and English.

"Miss Tami, look at this ad—it says: Japanese person who can speak as well as read and write English is needed,' but this is a tough position to fill." I said, since no one knows how to speak English, let alone read and write. *"Miss Tami, you would certainly qualify, but you need not work,"* I have stated.

In the meantime, I was strategizing an effective proposal points for the selling the necklace, emphasizing the necklace was custom designed and the stone was cut to complement the wearer, with brilliant fire. And the necklace featured an exquisite ten carats total weight in emeralds, held by a platinum chain with the emeralds and diamonds were inlaid in each chain's loop. I decided on an asking price of twenty thousand dollars, to be paid with U.S. currency, not the military scrip which substitutes the American dollar.

The next day, Miss Tami and I were back at the Mr. Ohara's shop, and he informed us that a potential buyer had been found. A tall distinguished looking middle-aged American officer entered the shop, accompanied by an interpreter. Miss Tami and I have noticed the officer had silver eagle studs on his epaulets and collar, which signified the rank of colonel; he must be the buyer for the necklace. After we have exchanged greetings, the interpreter informed that the colonel wished to see the diamond-and-emerald necklace.

I took out the folded black cloth from inside of my garment and revealed the brilliant piece of jewelry composed of emeralds and colorless diamonds. The diamonds sparked with lightning, and emeralds sparked with prisms of the rainbow, with a slightest movement of my hand.

"Exquisite! I can see with my naked eyes, this is flawless." The colonel commented, unable to take his eyes off the necklace. *"I wonder if this is a stolen good?"* The colonel made the accusatory comment; wondering out loud to himself, not know about the Miss Tami's knowledge of English.

"No, sir, this is my necklace, gifts from my mother, not stolen as you have surmised." Miss Tami replied with the perfect English. She had been quietly absorbing the situation until now and strongly refuted the colonel's accusation.

Surprised by Miss Tami's sudden enunciation, the colonel turned to look at her with an amazed expression.

"Young lady, where did you learn to speak such perfect English? You have no accent which most of our Japanese employees have, so that oftentimes I don't understand what was being said." The colonel said and added, *"My apologies, ma'am, but I was shocked to see such an exquisite piece of jewelry."* The colonel apologized, but Tami detected a slight skepticism in his demeanor.

"I see your doubt still remains. Allow me to enlighten you. However, your interpreter must excuse himself; tell him to be back in fifteen minutes." Miss Tami asked, and then, *"Before I begin, I must have your promise of strict secrecy. I don't wish to jeopardize my*

people's future by revealing how I came to possess this necklace." Miss Tami said, looking directly into the colonel's eyes. The officer recognized Miss Tami's uncompromising mien, and he nodded in agreement.

"You have my word of honor, not to breathe a word, ma'am." the colonel said assuredly, suppressing his mounting curiosity.

"My name is Tami Araki," she begun, I was born into a wealthy family, born late in my parents' life, as the only female child, and I have four adult brothers. The three oldest were executives in the family's real estate business, and the youngest went abroad as an exchange student to UCLA in Los Angeles, California, where he graduated with a degree in business." And then Miss Tami focused her subject mainly on how the extraordinary gems were in her position. Also she warned, Taka and her sister Yumi are her servants and bodyguards; moreover, don't underestimate them—if my life becomes threatened they, without a second thought, put their lives on the line, and the malevolent individual be assassinated. Please, don't doubt my words, Miss Tami ended her speech.

"Thank you, Miss Araki, for confiding in me. Your secret will not go any further than the spot I'm standing on. Also I will pay the asking price of this necklace, and I know my wife will be very pleased—so am I. But I need to transfer the funds from my bank in the States, which may take day or two. By the way, I'm Colonel Palmer, and I'm very pleased to make your acquaintance; I hope we'll see each other again." The colonel said paused for a moment, and then with a gentlemanly benevolence he kissed her hand.

The sale of the necklace had been concluded satisfactorily, and three days later, Miss Tami and I have left the busy and noisy city and headed back home.

Chapter 10: First Love

Leaning against the windowpane, Miss Tami had her eyes fixed on the distant landscape receding into the distance as the train sped past one village after another. And Miss Tami's mind was being pulled back along with the distant landscape to the sights and sounds of congested downtown Fukuoka, Unable to resist the persistent lure of Japan's, strange new postwar culture, which has captivated Miss Tami and she become as same as the younger generation.

Those young people were influenced by the free-spirited western milieu; and for the first time in their lives they did not answer to anyone. Instead they had revolted against the pressure of the strict feudalistic tradition and created a new lifestyle as they saw it fit. Ironically, they had entrapped themselves in a lawless misfit culture of their own making, becoming prisoners of their impotent ideas. However, Miss Tami did not accept going against authority, only welcomed freedom of being allowed to be herself.

Restoration of the Araki estate was now completed, and the grounds were beautifully landscaped just as the former estate was. The cemetery was added to where Miss Tami's teahouse was, and the ashes of Mistress Shizeka, father, and grandfather were buried and marked with black marble headstones with their names engraved in gold.

The year has turned and the first New Year to be celebrated at the newly rebuilt estate, and a plan was under way for the traditional ritual on the first day of the first month. Yumi has created the flower arrangements of three freshly cut portions of bamboo stalks, pine, and a branch of plum with the pink blossoms signifying glad tidings to welcome a prosperous New Year.

A few days prior to January the first, I was going to downtown Fukuoka to purchase necessary food items. Sake and red drum fish were on the traditional New Year's Day menu, and Mr. Ohara would have to purchase sake through his black market connections. Miss Tami decided to go along, not wanting to miss the chance to experience the exciting sights and sounds of the city, which she was unable to get out of her mind. When we entered Mr. Ohara's shop, he produced an envelope and handed it to Miss Tami. Informing *"Miss Araki, I have a message from Colonel Palmer for you. He came the day after you returned home and left this envelope addressed to you."*

Looking at the envelope addressed: To Miss Tami Araki.

"Thank you, Mr. Ohara; I wonder what this is all about?" Tami wondered out loud, staring at the envelope. *"Well, only one way to find out."* she said and took the letter out from the envelope.

Miss Araki:

Please accept my apology for presumptuously writing this letter. I have told Mrs. Palmer about you and your story, and she was most sympathetic, and admired your courage to survive, as I have. When we met, I was very impressed with your knowledge of the English language. This is not merely a friendly letter, however; I have a very serious request to present. As you know, people who can speak, read, and write English as well as Japanese are practically nonexistent. I do not know of any until I met you.

Perhaps you have realized by now that I am in dire need of a qualified assistant with whom I can communicate. Could you be that person for me? I do understand that you do not have to work, but please note, your salary and the benefits will far exceed that of Japanese executives. Also, all your needs will be met and paid for by an expense account, and you would have your own apartment on the base furnished by the Air Force, to accommodate your needs and comforts.

In addition, you will receive an annual Christmas bonus, which I will match with my own funds to double it.

I pray you will consider it.

Sincerely,

Colonel Jamison Palmer

PS: Mrs. Palmer loved the necklace—so much so that she wishes a pair of matching earrings. Can you help?

JP

Astonished by Colonel Palmer's message, Miss Tami felt as if she was the Cinderella, a fairy tale she read as a child; however, noticed my inquiring eyes, Miss Tami explained the colonel's message to me, and her own infatuation to the current culture of young people.

"Of course I will think it over very carefully, before making my

mind up to accept or to decline." Miss Tami said more to herself than to me.

"Miss Tami, I am very apprehensive about Colonel Palmer's offer; it sounds too good to be true, even though he appears to be a very nice man. But if you decide to accept his job offer, I'm coming with you as a personal maid and protector as I have been; moreover, I am as sure as sitting here, that many GIs will be mesmerized by your beauty and try to gain your favor, mark my words," I emphasized.

"Yes, Taka, many times your intuition has saved us from what could've been a life-threatening catastrophe, and you've been a mother to me in more ways than one; I'd be lost without you. We'll talk more later." Miss Tami promised.

Back at the Araki estate, we had long talk about Miss Tami's job, and both of us have agreed it's good for Miss Tami to be working. Miss Tami composed a letter of acceptance for Colonel Palmer, with the additional request that I will be her personal maid and bodyguard, handed the letter to Mr. Aoki at the New Year's Day dinner party, asking him to hand delivers the letter to the Colonel Palmer.

A few days later, Miss Tami received a letter from the colonel, informing the limousine would be sent for her and me on the designated date. Over the next few days, Miss Tami has excitedly prepared herself for the new life she would soon begin. When the limousine arrived, Miss Tami and I got in and sat side-by-side and room to spare, in the soft velvet backseat for ride to the base.

"Miss Tami, this big car, very quiet." I whispered, totally amazed by the smooth and silent limousine ride, in comparison to the train rides I was used to.

"Yes, Taka, I too am amazed. I suppose this is a part of the American lifestyle, and I could easily get used to it." Miss Tami confessed. A soothing beautiful melody flowed from the stereo

speakers, and the slight motion of the limousine felt as if they were riding on a cloud.

The limousine's slowing motion made Miss Tami to look out through the tinted windows, which keep the curious onlookers from trying to see into the interior.

There was a tall GI wearing a helmet with the letters MP was written, and he waved on to the driver, and limousine did not stop run through the gate. I saw the street devoid of pedestrians; only one or two military vehicles were going by on the wide paved road, so different from Japan's narrow, unpaved roads that were always congested. There was a wide sidewalk, just as wide as the roads of Japan, on each side of the street, and the clean buildings stood in the middle surrounded by a large, neatly landscaped perimeter.

"Miss Tami—ma'am, I don't feel like this is Japan?" I asked being mesmerized by what I saw.

"I agree, Taka. After passing through the gate, we are now in the occupied property of the United State of America, and ironically the Japanese citizens are prohibited free access, even though this is the country of Japan," Miss Tami explained.

The limousine stopped in front of a large building that had a walkway covered by a green canopy. At the front entrance was a sign read Zebra Club. This was the officers' club Colonel Palmer was in charge of, and Miss Tami was to be his assistant manager and private secretary.

As we entered the large foyer, Miss Tami's eyes immediately went to a large circular wet bar with a bartender stationed behind it. Miss Tami and I have never seen anything like this before. Behind the bar there was a mirrored wall reflecting the many liquor bottles of different shapes and colors lining four tiers of shelves. A variety of stemmed glasses hung upside down in a holder suspended from the ceiling; the holder resembled an upside-down table with long legs fastened to the ceiling.

Those glasses of many sizes and shapes were sparkling with twinkling tiny lights. The sight mesmerized Miss Tami; in fact the entire bar area was immersed in the slow-moving specks of light. It's a magic, she and I thought, recalling seeing the peacock's tail feathers spread open when Miss Tami was a child.

Captivated by the strange sea of lights, Miss Tami's searching eyes found a large ball covered with tiny mirrors. The ball was suspended from the ceiling and slowly turning as beams from high-intensity spotlights reflected off the mirrors.

"This way, ma'am." The limousine driver's sudden announcement has startled us, pulled our mind back from the fantasy of lights. She and I were led into a posh office with thick wall-to-wall pastel gray carpet, and there was a gleaming large ebony desk occupied one end of the room; which littered with paperwork, haphazardly strewn about. In the center of the room two large leather sofas were situated facing each other, with a glass-topped low table in between. On the coffee table was a large brandy stein full of chocolates wrapped in shiny foil.

A moment later, Colonel Palmer came out from his adjoining private room with a big smile.

"Miss Tami, Miss Taka, you have no idea how glad I am to see you," the colonel said, and he gathered us both in his arms and hugged emphatically; however, he was unaware of the girl's sudden cringe.

The customary Japanese greeting requires one must bow to show respect, never touch the other person; even children must bow to their parents and elders. Only the Americans would openly greet with hugs and kisses. Although we were greeted in such a manner, both of us has managed to hide embarrassment and tried to act natural.

Colonel Palmer sensed he has done something wrong, but clueless as to the reason why we were acting nervous. To cover the awkward feeling, the colonel has cheerfully announced, *"Ladies, I've taken the liberty of ordering lunch for us. I hope you like filet mignon."* The colonel then ushered us into the officers' dining room, which was immaculate, clean, and elegant; every table had a white linen tablecloth and a slender crystal vase holding a single long-stemmed red rose placed in a center.

We were nervous; never have been in such a spacious dining room and having no idea what filet mignon was. But Miss Tami did not have the courage to ask, what filet mignon is. When the food arrived, to our pleasant surprise, we have sampled tender morsels of beef broiled to perfection.

"This meat was shipped from Stateside for the club's use only. How did you like it?" the colonel asked.

"It was very good, sir. Neither of us had eaten meat, only heard about it before the war. Thank you for the most delicious lunch, we've enjoyed it very much," Miss Tami expressed her gratitude.

"I'm pleased." Colonel Palmer was genuinely elated, and had a sense of whatever he had done wrong earlier had now been forgiven.

After the meal all of us have enjoyed sipping fragrant cups of hot coffee. It was our first taste of coffee, and we were addicted to the indescribably delicious coffee.

Colonel Palmer has brought up the subject of Miss Tami's job, asking her to remain at the base until after the contract was signed. In the meantime, officers and families have begun arriving for luncheon, and for the first time we saw the blond-haired children who had porcelain-white skin and large blue eyes, Miss Tami has seen in her fairy-tale book when she was a child. However, Miss Tami did not see the stares of the officers who were mesmerized by exquisite Oriental beauty.

The limousine drove through a quiet residential section of the base and pulled up in front of a four-story apartment complex. The colonel escorted us into an elevator, and we ascended to the second floor and to the apartment 201. Upon entering the spacious apartment, we were walking soundlessly on a thick beige carpet, and through the ceiling-to-floor sliding glass door we saw the sweeping green fairway, but we did not know this was a golf course.

"Come, ladies." The colonel urged the awestruck us to show the apartment's interior layout and furnishing. The master bedroom was furnished with a brand-new queen-size bed and easy chair, vanity with matching chair, and mirrored dresser. The second bedroom had a double bed. Each bedroom had its own bathroom, and colonel thought we needed coaching before we understood how the facilities worked.

"Miss Tami, I think I'm dreaming?" I said in disbelief, and then we were led to the kitchen equipped with a large refrigerator as tall as the colonel Palmer, a gas stove with four burners and oven, and white porcelain double sink with hot and cold running water; and needs only to turn the faucet on.

"Now I know I'm dreaming," I said. For the first time in my life I had hot and cold running water in the house. *"Miss Tami, do you know how to use this cooking machine?"* I whispered.

"I don't know, but I'll find out." Miss Tami said, but without appearing ignorant, she said, *"Colonel Palmer, the apartment is grand, I thank you very much; however, Taka has never used an appliance such as this one."* Miss Tami indicated the stove.

"Oh, it's easy to use. This is a stove, and those are the four burners." The colonel pointed his finger, but we were more puzzled by the stove.

I could not comprehend how the stove would work, picturing

myself burning wood on top of the stove to cook a meal? *"That's awful! This beautiful apartment will be filled with smoke. I don't think I like this stove."* I whispered to Miss Tami.

Colonel Palmer did not have any inkling as to my confusion; he went on to explain further. *"This is an oven,"* He opened the oven door and closed it to show how it worked.

"What does the oven do, sir? How do I make fire on this cooking machine?" I asked, more puzzled and wished never saw a stove; Miss Tami relayed my question to the colonel.

"Forgive me, Taka, see these knobs? Push in and turn it to the right," the colonel instructed. I pushed a knob in as I was directed, and then slowly turned not realizing what would happen. POUF! A circle of blue flames shot up from the burner, I jumped back. We were surprised, and more I turned the knob the greater the flames were.

"Heavens! This is magic. I never saw anything like it. Look, no smoke!" I exclaimed.

At that moment, the colonel made a mental note to have a talk with Mrs. Palmer, and send their maid over to show Taka how to use the appliances such as the washer, dryer, vacuum cleaner, and give her some cooking tips.

We stayed in our beautiful posh apartment, feeling strange in this new environment, but *"I can get used to it!"* Miss Tami expressed her sentiment with a smile.

"Miss Tami, this is very, ahhh—so beautiful I can't believe I have the right to live here, ma'am. When I think of many people were living in a street, make shift hut." I said, trying to justify my mixed feelings of titillating guilt.

"Don't be Taka, it is a, and I too am feel strange, actually I am to live in a beautiful apartment. Perhaps we jumped suddenly into the new culture without being acclimated. I hope I have not made a mistake."

"Miss Tami, I don't know what tomorrow will bring, but please do not fear, I will be at your side as always."

"I know; I feel safe knowing you are with me."

"Ma'am, this apartment is very nice. I will make certain you'll be happy here." I have assured Miss Tami.

The golden opportunity of a lifetime was handed to Miss Tami on a silver platter, and she signed the contract after the detailed stipulations were discussed and agreed upon. Miss Tami became an employee of the United States Air Force, and her starting salary was ten thousand American dollars a year, an unheard-of sum in Japan at that time. Also, she would receive biannual pay raises, Christmas bonus, free medical insurance, paid vacation, and expense allowances all amenities which did not exist in the Japanese workforce. Miss Tami was to begin her work in two weeks.

Miss Tami and I were invited to dine at the Zebra Club with Colonel Palmer and his wife, and the limousine came to pick us up. After the round of introductions, Mrs. Palmer was no longer able to hold herself back, and said,

"Miss Araki, you are the most beautiful young lady I've met since I came to Japan. Jamison told me how beautiful you are, but all the young girls are beautiful to him so I didn't pay any mind, only this time I agreed." Mrs. Palmer said smiling, unable to takes her eyes off Miss Tami.

"Thank you, ma'am, I am honored." Miss Tami replied, but embarrassed by the praise received she did not know how or where to hide her blushed face. Mrs. Palmer realized she has caused Miss Tami to be ill at ease, quickly changed the subject.

"I am so glad you came to work for my husband. You have no idea how frustrated he was not having a competent secretary. Hopefully having you will get my sane husband back," Mrs. Palmer confessed.

"I will be the best and most competent secretary the colonel deserves. Ma'am," Tami replied sincerely.

Tami and I have returned to the estate to pack, but Tami did not have the appropriate clothes to wear as a respectable secretary. There was also the question of who would manage the estate, and after giving it careful thought, Tami appointed Yumi to handle all the responsibilities. She gathered the servants together to explain that she would be working as Colonel Palmer's secretary, so she has left the estate to live in the base, and from now on Yumi would be the headmaster. The servants were emotional and upset by the news, but they swore to respect her wish faithfully. Tenshi began whimpering as if he understood, and he stayed close to his mistress. Tami sat down with him stroking softly as she whispered how much she loved him. He put his head on Tami's lap, savoring her tender touch.

The call from an MP informing Miss Tami and I were at the gate, which surprised the colonel Palmer, and we needed to be verified. Immediately Colonel Palmer sent a staff car to pick us up. After hearing the reason for our early arrival was to purchase ensembles from the PX to wear as a colonel's respectable secretary, because there was no other shop in town retailing respectable clothing's.

The colonel telephoned Mrs. Palmer to meet Tami at her apartment explaining the reason for their an early arrival, Promptly Mrs. Palmer was at an apartment, informing we were going to shopping at the PX, and the three of us headed out to the PX in Mrs. Palmer's Jaguar. I was sitting in back, awed by the smooth ride, just as smooth as the big limousine, and thinking I like this car!

We returned with the car trunk was full of housekeeping needs, everything from pots and pans to groceries, armloads of new clothes and accessories for Miss Tami. *"You'll look nice dear, sitting at the front desk."*

Mrs. Palmer commented with a smile, proud of her selections for Miss Tami. Tami thanked Mrs. Palmer for her generous gifts, since she had no idea how to shop for clothes.

Thanks to Mrs. Palmer's maid, I have learned a new way of housekeeping. Although it was difficult at first, but I learn how to use the power appliances and the housekeeping was joyful, an each time I used the brand-new pots and pans, stove, vacuum cleaner, and the washer/dryer which were heaven sent, and the American way of housekeeping was an adventure I have never dreamt of.

Miss Tami started to work, when two officers walked into the reception room and asked Miss Tami to announce their arrival to the colonel. One of the younger officers did a double take after one look at Miss Tami, as they sat down on the sofa facing the desk, Miss Tami gave him a nod and smile, noticing how handsome he was, and her heart begun beating rapidly as she watched the two officers went into Colonel Palmer's private office.

"Miss Araki, come into my office." Colonel Palmer's voice came through the intercom.

Quickly Tami glanced at herself in her compact mirror, patted her nose with a make-up pad, ran her fingers through her hair and then shook it to fall naturally on her shoulders. And then she took a deep breath, exhaled slowly to calm herself, before she enter into the colonel's office.

"My, you look lovely!" The colonel said, awed by Tami's sudden transformation since this morning.

The two officers stood up, and Colonel Palmer introduced Tami to his colleagues, and they were associated with the Zebra Club's business, shook hands with Miss Tami, spellbound by her mystic beauty unable to take their eyes off of her, especially the younger of the two.

His name was Lieutenant James Courtland. He was tall and handsome, standing head and shoulders taller than Miss Tami, and as the lieutenant held her hand an electrifying shock shot up her arm. Tami stood as if a mannequin in store window, unable to look at his face, knowing she was blushed crimson.

The awestruck lieutenant has inevitably held onto Tami's hand longer than a gentleman's etiquette allowed, but he felt a slight tug of her hand jarred his senses.

"I beg your pardon." The lieutenants apologized, but with Tami's dreamy smiling eyes staring into his redden face and deep blue eyes, instantly he felt a deep affinity for her. From that day on Lieutenant Courtland stopped by the Zebra Club as frequently as a homing pigeon, making up one reason or another as an excuse to see Tami.

James always held his emotion in check when he came into the reception room. It was obvious that he has created a chance to see Miss Tami, although only an exchange of a smile or just say *"Hi! How are you."* In a passing, however, James did not see beyond Miss Tami's beautiful face was a well-hidden tormenting pain of being in love for the first time.

Every day Miss Tami was on pins and needles, trying to suppress her loudly beating heart, anxiously waiting for the lieutenant to walk through the door, but every day after exchanging a casual "Hi, how are you," or just "Hi" and melt-your-heart smile, he was gone as quickly as he came. Even then Tami was rapturously happy, floating on a cloud, holding onto his handsome smile and the lingering sound of his sexy voice. Those brief encounters has enabled her to get through the day, but every weekend was tortuous; Tami spent forty-eight hours in agony, while everyone else was having a good time or just relaxing, Tami's heart ached waiting for Monday to come and bring her another magical moment of seeing the love of her life, the incredibly handsome Lieutenant Courtland.

James Courtland has twin brother named Thomas, and they grew up in the orphanage since they were toddlers, and they did not know their parents. There were few more children lived there, who did not know the parents. When James and Thomas graduated from high school, James has enlisted in the Air Force, and he went through thirteen and half weeks of training, and upon graduation James was accepted to the Air Force academy, judged by his high scored an aptitude test. And he had four years of schooling on a scholarship, graduated with a rank of the second Lieutenant, and he was sent to Japan as an Air Force Officer.

Thomas, his twin brother was interested in an art, and drafting, and he got a job at an advertising agency upon graduating from high school, working in mailroom, receiving minimal pay and worked himself up as a blue print apprentice.

At the age of seventeen, for the first time, Miss Tami was experiencing the bittersweet pain of being in love imagining desperately to be held in James's arms, having his lips on her soft lips. I have noticed the change in Miss Tami's demeanor…her loss of appetite, mood swings, and she has begun to wear make-up, trying to make herself look older than a young teenager.

Miss Tami was in love, I knew the sign. Bless her heart, she needs her mother and her wisdom; I must approach her on Mistress Shizuka's behalf to help this important and delicate time of passage in her life. Hopefully she will open up to me. I know Miss Tami's dilemma was serious not to be taken lightly. One evening, we were having diner, a chance I have been waiting has presented itself, instead of clearing the table I approached Miss Tami I brought up the subject.

"Miss Tami, I must speak to you about a matter that is worrying me sick, ma'am," I begun. Miss Tami was surprised, but she gave her permission to speak. *"What I'm about to say is only your mother has the right, but I must speak to you on her behalf."* I then went on to express the reasons for her concern.

"I realize you have grown up during the war, and all the young men of your age were taken to war, and you've never had a male friend of your own age. It is hard enough being in love, but the first time is even harder, because you have entered adulthood at the tender age of seventeen. It can be a cruel dilemma, but it will be helpful if you would talk about it. Please, ma'am, tell me about your young man; he must be a fine man to capture your heart."

I had my eyes on Miss Tami's pale face, praying Mistress Shizuka's wisdom would help to guide Miss Tami through this formidable period of her life.

Miss Tami was silent while listening to me, she must have felt a huge burden was left off her shoulder, as though a floodgate has opened to release her pain of be in love but unable to talk about it.

She began to talk about Lieutenant James Courtland. After a good talk with Miss Tami, I assured being in love was a normal part of a growing up, and some people will experience many more times. Relieved of what had been eating her alive, Miss Tami felt better as well as enlightened, and she felt hungry. Immediately I have reheated the evening meal, watched her consume diner with damp eyes, knowing Miss Tami's first crisis had passed.

However, the relationship between Miss Tami and Lieutenant Courtland was going nowhere; still they have exchanged a short greeting of *"Hello"* and *"How are you"* in passing, and then as usual, in a matter of moment the lieutenant was gone, leaving Tami with another painful twenty-four hours.

Although Miss Tami and I did not know James was also

tormented by being in love for the first time. He and his twin brother had grown up in an orphanage, and boys had to abide by strict house rule, either James or Thomas had a chance to meet a girl or fall in love. But for a first time in his life he was helplessly in love with a Japanese girl, against the strict Air Force regulations, forbidding relationships between GIs and Japanese females.

The reason given for the prohibition was that the GI could be shipped off at any time, leaving his girlfriend behind never to see her again...And God forbid if there was a child involved. Already there were many such half-breeds whom the Japanese government would not recognize as a citizen of Japan, so those children had no surnames or birth certificates. Moreover, they were treated as an outcasts, and child's Japanese families or the society did not accepts as their blood, because of the shame brought on by a half-bleed.

Many a night James fought with his desire to confess his love to Tami, in fear he would be shipped out when his relationship with Miss Tami became known, and he would have no choice but to leave Miss Tami behind. Though there was one solution and it was risky, but James decided to take that risk and called on the base chaplain.

In the privacy of the chapel office, James told the chaplain everything from the beginning, and added he had not told Tami that he loved her. When the chaplain gave his advice, it was contrary to what James had been expecting, surprised James. The chaplain said, *"After listening to you, I see clearly you are a thoughtful gentleman. If I was you, I wouldn't wait for another minute to tell the young lady how much I loved her,"* chaplain emphasized.

The chaplain's advice was extraordinary; James thanked him and headed straight to the Zebra Club.

Miss Tami was in a near faint, when she saw Lieutenant Courtland, who has been absent from the club for a week, suddenly he was standing in front of her. Miss Tami believed his long absence meant he was either been shipped out or he no longer wanted to see her; in any case she was dying a slow death, but now not only had he come back, but also he asked her to have coffee with him.

Miss Tami has accepted his invitation immediately, and sprung up from her chair to accompany the lieutenant in the club dining room. There they sat quietly together, nervously sipping coffee. Lieutenant Courtland was especially nervous and fidgety and unable to contain himself.

"Forgive me, sir, but is there a something's matter Lieutenant?" Miss Tami asked.

"No, Miss Araki, just that sitting so close to you makes me dizzy," the lieutenant confessed. The lieutenant's impromptu utterance made it obvious that his words came from his heart.

Miss Tami put her coffee cup down and gathered her courage reached out to take the lieutenant's hand, and looked into his clear blue eyes, said,

"So am I, Lieutenant." At that moment both realized how deeply they were in love.

"It's too crowded here…Would you take a ride with me?" James asked, and together they walked out of the Zebra Club to where he parked his jeep, and then suddenly James scooped Miss Tami up and sat her down in front seat of the jeep. Miss Tami told me that, all she remembered was leaving the club and riding in a jeep next to him, while he held her hand, only to letting go so he could shift the gears. Miss Tami was feeling his pulsating heartbeat flowing right into her heart through his warm large hand.

If I am dreaming…Please…I don't want to wake up. She thought, and breeze cooled off her hot face.

"Are you okay, Miss Araki?" the lieutenant asked.

"Yes, I'm fine. Please, call me Tami." Being so close to him, she was intoxicated by the scent of the lieutenant's aftershave.

"Miss Tami, I must speak to you about, a … an important matter I need to tell you." James said as he drove. And then he said.

"Call me James."

"Yes, James." Miss Tami responded, suggesting her apartment will be more private.

I was in my bedroom reading a Japanese magazine, Mrs. Palmer has bought for me, when Miss Tami came home in the middle of the day with an incredibly handsome tall officer, I was surprised to see Miss Tami and an officer, and she introduced me as Lieutenant Courtland; immediately I understood the situation and quietly excused myself to bedroom.

"Miss Tami, what I'm about to tell you is very important, for both of us." "Ever since I first saw you at the Zebra Club, you have been on my mind day and night, and for the first time in my life, I have fallen head over heels in love with you. But if we permitted ourselves to be in love, I am certain to be shipped off and we'll never see each other again, and you could be dismissed from your job. It is our government's policy to break up the relationships. Not only I have refrained from seeing you, but at the same time I was driving myself mad. So I sought the help of Chaplain Major Wyandt, and told him everything, except I have not told you that I loved you. I had to be doubly cautious approaching this delicate situation."

James stopped and looked at Miss Tami, who had not said a word, and he saw tears sparkling in her eyes. He gathered Miss Tami in his arms and whispered, *"I love you Miss Tami."*

"James, I-I—" Before Miss Tami could finish her sentence, James's lips were on hers and he kept whispering, "I love you, Tami, I love you," holding her trembling body, unable to stop himself from telling Miss Tami how much he loved her.

Being held in his arms, Miss Tami was actually felt his warm body; for once she was content with her handsome young lieutenant, and the fresh scent of his deodorant assured her that it was no longer a wishful fantasy she dreamt of every waking moment and in her dream. From that moment the tormenting pain in her heart vanished, and Miss Tami blossomed just as a lovely rose opened up.

Over the coming days, Miss Tami has suddenly become radiantly beautiful, and her eyes sparkled as she smiled. James began picking her up to take her to and from work, so Colonel Palmer's driver's service was no longer needed also Lieutenant Courtland's frequent visits to the Zebra Club has ceased.

Putting two and two together, Colonel Palmer knew Miss Tami and Lieutenant Courtland were in love, this was not good news for the colonel, because he suspected that their marriage was imminent, and he would lose Miss Tami, his most valued employee. Not only she has managed the Zebra Club, but also the colonel's personal affairs as well; he could not afford to lose Miss Tami girl who kept his life in order and acted as his better half in the office. Without Miss Tami colonel could not function, so colonel decided to put a stop to their love affair on a sly.

Lieutenant Cortland knew he was breaking Air Force's code of law, getting involved with a Japanese girl; yet the lieutenant has fallen in love, against strict rule. Before James could propose marriage to Tami, he needed a confirmation of the engagement from his commanding general, and needed the general's signature on the affidavit; however, that was easier said than done. Again Lieutenant Cortland has appealed to the chaplain, asking if he would meet with Miss Tami.

"I will be pleased to meet with your young lady." The chaplain said, putting James's mind at ease.

The Lieutenant and Miss Tami held each other's hand, as

they nervously sat in the chapel, waited for Chaplain Wyandt. The report of this interview would be the deciding factor enables them to further their marriage requisition.

"*Miss Araki, Lieutenant Courtland, please come in.*" The chaplain's secretary said, gestured for them to come in the chaplain's office, he was sitting behind his desk.

The chaplain was looking at Tami, completely mesmerized by this beautiful Japanese girl, and with a grandfatherly smile on his face he began talking to her, encouraging her to tell him about herself.

After hearing the horrifying story of Miss Tami's extraordinary life, the chaplain was silent. They both realized for the first time, incredibly three young girls has survived through the war without any adult guidance or protection.

"*You were only a child when orphaned and became homeless.*" The chaplain said. "*Moreover, it is incredible to me that you do not have a hint of animosity for having to live through the horror of war, and then how you have educated yourself to such a caliber is beyond me. Lieutenant Courtland, take good care of this lady, or you will have me to answer to. By the way, look me up if you two happen to be in my neighborhood, Fort Wayne, Indiana. My Mrs. and I will be glad to invite you two for dinner; she makes the best fried chicken.*" The chaplain concluded with a smile.

Leaving the chapel, James was silent and had a serious expression on his face. Miss Tami felt uneasy, seeing James was upset. I must've said something to upset him, she thought, as she went over the interview with the chaplain in her mind.

"*James, please speak to me. I can see you are very upset; was it something I said to the chaplain?*" Miss Tami asked, almost in tears.

"*Oh no, darling, you were charming and wonderful. Let's go back to your apartment, I'll explain.*" James said hugged Tami.

Chapter 11: Forbidden Matrimony

Seeing James and Miss Tami's serious demeanor, when they entered the apartment, I knew something very serious was up, quietly I left the room. As the couple sat side by side on the sofa, James tried his best to explain to Miss Tami without frightening her about the existing situation.

The American government would not approve of a relationship between a GI and a Japanese girl, the reason being, her future life with a GI lover she would be subjected to disrespectful treatment, and obtaining the grant for a marriage would be nearly impossible.

More often than not, the Japanese wife was outcast by her own family for not upholding her traditional culture, and marrying a foreigner without the family's consent. Through no fault of her own she would be shunned by her own family and her husband's friends, because she had fallen in love with an American GI.

"Miss Tami, I am afraid I have led you into harm's way," James began. And he said, *"Sit next to me."* James said, and he gathered Miss Tami's slight body in his arms and told her of the seemingly

heartless government tactic of forbidding relationships between GIs and Japanese girls.

"*But, James, how could the American government do this to us girls? Do I pose some kind of danger for loving you? Please tell me it's not true.*" Miss Tami pleaded, staring intensely into James's blue eyes.

"*You see, Tami, when we landed in Japan, the first order given to us was under no circumstance never to become involved with the Japanese girls, not even as casual friends.*" Pausing for a moment, James recalled the time when his commanding officer was drilling the message into all the newly arrived GIs, and we all thought, not to do what?

But why? Am I not good enough and still being considered as an enemy?" Tami asked, and she was clearly shaken.

"*Oh no, my darling. Our government's intention was to prevent emotional devastation to the innocent young Japanese girls,*" because the relationships had no future. Sooner or later, all the GIs will be sent to some other location and could happened at any time…or he will be discharged and return home or to his girlfriend, to his waiting wife, his family, and often he will no longer think or care about the Japanese girl he left behind and the proof everywhere. None of us knew about the cultural differences existing between Japan and the U.S. We didn't know the girl could not return home after she was abandoned, because she has brought shame to her family. Often time these situations have ended tragically.

"*How do you know about this?*" Miss Tami asked, shaken by such information.

"*My brother Thomas sent newspaper clippings, after I have told him about you, and I am hoping to marry her.*"

A young Japanese wife named Kimiyo came to Chicago with her two small children and her GI husband, and she had hopes and dreams of being a family, but everything Kimiko has expected, as being a wife and mother, was ignored by her husband, who no longer felt lonely since he was home with his loved ones.

"But James, this GI, he loved her enough to marry …" Tami was threatened by the story, and she could not finish the sentence.

The truth of the matter was, his Japanese wife and children did not fit his lifestyle in the U.S., and they became a burden to him, and to his family. Her in-laws shunned their Japanese daughter-in-law and their grandchildren, because they looked different. Some of their relatives still considered her as an enemy.

The English language was unfamiliar to her, and she knew only a pidgin, broken English, which she picked up from her husband, he spoke to her so she would understand. But the English spoken in the U.S. was different, although she understood most of what was being said, and she tried to speak the only way she knew how, and she was blatantly ridiculed as stupid for talking in pidgin, means broken English, Kimiko also could not operate the appliances, because she did not know how and could not ask for a help.

Moreover, no one would lend a hand to show her how to do things; instead, they openly criticized everything she did or did not do, they were convinced she did not understand what was being said around her.

Her mother-in-law told neighbors and acquaintances how stupid she was and added, *"That girl don't even know how to use stove and ironing board, and everything else in the house,"* to anybody who would listen.

That girl, she called her, never referred to Kimiko by her name, because none of in-laws could correctly pronounce her name or remembered her name.

"She's so dumb, can't talk right. You utta' watch her try to clean

the house…She don't know how a' use vacuum cleaner, or anything else. And those kids, I don't want them in my house." The mother-in-law kept complaining, but unfortunately Kimiko did not know enough English to speak up. Irony of it all Kimiko did not know she had an ally.

It was a next-door neighbor, who felt sorry for Kimiyo, and told her mother-in-law when she again begun to complain about Kimiko. *"Listen."* The neighbor woman said to Kimiko's in-law, if you went to Japan and did not speak or understand their language, can you understand what was said and do things their way? And people call you a stupid?' After that remark, the girl's mother-in-law kept her mouth shut most of the time.

Kimiko understood she and the children were unwelcome intruders, and she begged her husband to get an apartment. But her plea fell on deaf ears, and he behaved as if he was a carefree bachelor. So one day, out of desperation, she planned a tea party with her children, and mixed rat poison and sugar in the tea, killing the children, but she survived and was hospitalized. After Kimiko has regained her health and discharged from the hospital, judge has ruled the children's death was an accidental, considering the circumstance, and she was deported without being charged. However, after she was back in Japan, what might have happed to her was anyone's guess James told to Miss Tami.

Most of those marriages has ended in divorce, and when the woman was no longer able to live at her in-laws' house, and she could not speak correct English getting a job was impossible, she had no alternative but to became a homeless prostitute. There was a law required every GI has to sign an affidavit, stating case of an emergency or divorce, he had enough money in the bank to pay for her way home. In an end though, most of them didn't have the money or ignored their responsibility and looked the other way.

"However, a minute percent of such marriages have succeed, and these couples became parents living happily ever after," James concluded.

Tami was silent and had a serious look on her face with her eyes downcast, while James waited for her to say something.

"I heard every word you spoke, but, my darling James, I love you no matter the circumstances. I also know you would never abandon me." Miss Tami whispered and buried herself in his tender hug.

"If ever a time would come for your government to take you away from me, I will be with you in spirit because I have no desire to live without you," Miss Tami said somberly. That statement caught James off guard; he pulled himself away enough to look at Miss Tami's face.

"What did you mean by that?" James asked, but he knew the implication of her words.

"I meant I have no desire to live without you," Tami repeated.

"I love you, dear. I don't know of any other way to tell you, but to say I love you." James whispered with his face pressed against her soft cheek.

James had requested the marriage application he needed to submit to his commanding general, and the following week h be received several pages of forms to be completed. Only when these forms were signed by his commanding officer, the marriage affidavit will be valid.

James did not have any problem with getting his paperwork completed since the Air Force had all the needed information, but Tami had to be investigated by the Japanese secret police, by order of the Headquarters Far East Air Forces, the Inspector General, Offices of Special Investigations, District Office #4 AFO 929.

Tami was subjected to repeated interviews, and physical examinations, had to produce written character references from her family's acquaintances, friends, schoolteachers, and the local shopkeepers. Those were the most difficult tasks since many had fled or perished during the war. She also had to undergo a psychiatric analysis to find any possible flaws in her personality. Even with the difficulties James and Tami made progress, in spite of the impediment superimposed by the U.S. government to delay the furtherance of their marriage quest.

One weekend, James and Miss Tami were enjoying a rare moment of relaxation at her apartment, but Tami noticed James was somewhat nervous.

"Something is bothering you. What is it, James?" she asked.

"Tami, darling, I have been trying to come up with an appropriate way of asking you to marry me. I should've asked you first, but I had to have the permission from my commanding general. Miss Tami, will you marry me?" James asked, not realizing how hard he was gripping Tami's hands.

"Oh, yes, James, as long as you'll have me," Tami whispered. She really wanted to shout to the world, but instead she flung her arms around James's neck and wept.

James did not yet have an engagement ring for Tami. He went to the PX to find an appropriate ring, and then to the black market, but could not find a ring worthy of Tami. James then decided to have his brother Thomas, who lived in Los Angeles, search for a jeweler, and he described the ring he had in mind. Tami, however, had another idea; she suggested James accompany her to the estate in the near future, explaining she wished to show him her mother's gems, and one day they made the surprise homecoming. Tami asked Yumi to bring her black lacquer jewelry box, and as Yumi placed the box in her mistress's hands, Tami then handed the box to James asking him to open it, and as he did James nearly dropped the box.

In all of his life, James had never seen such precious gems totaling millions of dollars, and now he was actually holding them in his hands. After his shock subsided and he regained his wits, he and Tami began to examine the diamonds together. They chose the stones appropriate for her engagement ring, and Tami chose one for him. At first James was hesitant to accept such an extraordinary gift, but Tami was adamant, telling him, *"Please, James, these rings will be a token of our love for each other. It's a gift from my mother and me, and I know she would be pleased. So am I,"* Tami insisted.

James accepted with gratitude, and they agreed that both of their engagement rings would have a five-carat emerald-cut diamond with quarter-carat solitaire amethysts on each side, all set in an eighteen-karat gold band.

Tami and James left the estate, and soon they approached what had once been a farming village. The village was still mostly piles of debris, but had a few crudely erected dwellings of salvaged charred wood. Stopping at the roadside for a moment, Tami explained about the bombing raid and how the remains of the deceased were still buried under the debris; hearing this was an eye-opening experience for James.

Upon returning to the base, immediately James shipped the gems by express air mail to his brother Thomas, to have the rings made by a reputable jeweler; and he preferred an old family establishment located on Hill Street in downtown Los Angeles.

Everything was progressing without a hitch, and then late one night shortly after James proposed to Miss Tami, there was rapid knocks on the apartment door woke Tami and me. *"Who is it, please?"* I asked, suppressing my rapidly pounding heart.

"Taka, it's me, James. Please open the door, I need to see Tami." James's voice sounded frantic. Miss Tami came running out of the

bedroom and swung open the door before James even finished the sentence, and there stood James wearing battle fatigues and boots as if he was on his way to war.

"Darling, I am being sent to Korea." James said, gathering Tami in his arms. Dumbstruck by his shocking statement, Tami was unable to speak, a big lump in her throat.

"Listen, Tami. No matter how long I'm gone or how far away I'm being sent, I will be as close to you as I am now with all my love. I'll be back after my tour is over."

"H-how long?" Miss Tami asked, but her voice sounded like a whisper, coming through with a lump in her throat.

"Eighteen months. Forgive me, my love, for leaving you. I knew this was coming, but I hoped it wouldn't happen so soon." James continued, but the sound of a car horn interrupted him.

"I have to go, Tami. The transport will be leaving in twenty minutes from Itazuke, but the guys were kind enough to let me come by to see you before I left." James said and passionately kissed Miss Tami and hugged her trembling body, and then he was gone. Miss Tami stood where James was a moment ago, unable to move.

"Come, Miss Tami, you'll catch a chill standing barefooted." I said, urged the grief-stricken Miss Tami to her bedroom and helped into bed. But without James was unbearable, Miss Tami could not stop sobbing.

Since James has left, long days and nights lingered, as the minutes and hours were locked in time. Miss Tami's sole thought was on the day James would walk in through the apartment door. Working daily provided only a minuscule diversion from her excruciating heartache and loneliness, corresponding with James was their lifeline to assure each other that counting down the days until they would be together again.

The Colonel Palmer has pulled rank, an underhanded way to

derail James and Miss Tami's imminent marriage, which neither of them knew, but his tactic was failing not a pint of a hint of their love fading. Apparently the colonel's delaying tactic has to be changed, to stop them in their tracks, unable to swallow a thought of losing Tami to that handsome young lieutenant; Colonel Palmer was even more determined to put a stop to James and the Miss Tami's marriage.

Until now he had never thought another female would come into his heart, no matter how attractive the girl happened to be, but Miss Tami stirred his forgotten feelings. Mrs. Palmer has sensed her husband's aloofness, and she thought to herself,

"A puppy love at his age, for goodness' sake!" The wise woman knew her husband well, and understood he would cool off soon enough.

An early one morning there was knocks on the apartment door, the moment Miss Tami had been desperately waiting for. She jumped out of her bed, ran and threw open the door, jumped into James's open arms, locked in an each other's arms; they devoured each other with kisses.

"I dreamt and lived for this moment every day, for 547 days. I missed you, my beautiful Tami." James whispered, and then suddenly he scooped Miss Tami up, carried her into the living room, put her down on the sofa, and he sat next to her.

"James, many a night I have prayed that when I woke the year and a half would be gone, and you'd be at my side. Darling, you are truly here I'm not dreaming, am I?" Miss Tami said, hugging James's neck.

"You are not dreaming, love, and neither am I? We'll never be apart again." James's voice carried his strong conviction.

"Welcome home, Lieutenant Courtland. We are very happy to have you back, sir." I greeted the Lieutenant, knowing Miss Tami's agony was over.

"Tami, I hate to leave you, but I need to go to my quarters. I'll be back to pick you up. We have lots to do." James said, he hugged Miss Tami and kissed her soft lips, but this time he would be right back.

Rapturously happy, Miss Tami was soaking in a warm bath to calm herself and be ready when James returned, when James returned he was wearing the blue Class A. dress uniform and how handsome he looked, having acquired a golden tan while he was stationed in Korea.

"You are more handsome than I remembered." Miss Tami said admiringly, looking up at the man for whom she has waited painfully long time.

"Tami, you are the one glowing with beauty, and each time I look at you my heart beats hard. I've counted each passing day for this moment," James confessed.

Tami and James stopped by the Zebra Club to inform Colonel Palmer that she needed a day off to take care of their personal business because the marriage documents James had prepared while in Korea had to be turned in. As they were leaving Colonel Parmer came out from the inner office.

Tami turned and saw his ashen face. *"Are you okay, sir?"* She asked, but the colonel did not answer, only stared. Miss Tami and James would never know the true reason for colonel's silence.

A week has passed since the marriage acquisition documents were turned in, but James and Miss Tami has not received the single page of signed affidavit by the commanding general and James was concerned. And then the documents were returned with INVALID stamped on.

James made a call to the commanding officer's office, trying desperately to find out the reason, but an each time his called, his call was put on hold and then he hear a sound of busy signal adding insult to his aggravation the phone goes dead.

Stupefied but determined to get to the truth of the matter, James stormed into the commanding general's office unannounced, only to be stymied by the desk sergeant's lame runaround, the affront was insult to his intelligent and pushed James to the limit of patience, he became furious, but realize he was caught in a malicious premeditated deadlock, and he had no idea where to go from here, and confided in Miss Tami about what had been happening.

After listening to James, Miss Tami pointed out that James had all the paperwork done in Korea, maybe that was the problem. But James knew that should not have any adverse effects as far as preparation of the documents, were only need the commanding officer's signature, so again he appealed to the base chaplain.

After hearing their puzzling predicament, the chaplain suspected the source of malignity, and he was most sympathetic to James. He has updated his letter of recommendation of Lieutenant and Miss Tami's marriage, the chaplain has added P.S. which read, "Without undue delay, complete the marriage affidavit requested by Lieutenant James T. Courtland and Miss Tami Araki." And then chaplain handed the signed and sealed letter to James.

Immediately James went straight to the commanding general's office and handed the letter to the desk sergeant, reminding him of the urgency and process the affidavit at once. The desk sergeant was not in any big hurry, took the envelope containing the letter from the chaplain, haphazardly put it aside, and returned to read Stars and Stripes news paper.

BANG! A fist came down on the sergeant's desk, causing the telephone receiver to rattle, the sergeant dropped his newspaper and sat bolt upright in his seat, and he saw the look of murder in the lieutenant's eyes. *"Have you not heard me? I said this is urgent!"* James said, strongly emphasizing each word, barely suppressing his anger and an urge to shout. But he has swallowed the words never to say it again, he has promised to nun back when he was a naughty little boy.

"I-I was ordered to-to…" The sergeant said his shaking voice trailed off.

"What, what order? From whom?" James planted both his hands on the desk, bent down and leveled himself to the sergeant. *"I repeat. Hear me—what did you say just now?"*

"I can't say it, sir. I'm not at liberty to reveal—sorry." the sergeant said lamely shedding his devil-may-care attitude, and again he said, *"Sorry, sir."*

Within a week of the encounter with the desk sergeant, all the paperwork was signed, sealed, and hand delivered by the sergeant.

What's in the hell's going on? A thought shot across James's mind, but instead he shouted *"Hallelujah!"* and made a beeline to pick Miss Tami up at work.

Tami took one look at James when he burst into the club, and she knew. *"I'm going to take a break, sir,"* she hollered in the direction of Colonel Palmer's office and ran out the door without waiting for the colonel's response, and she and James were headed for the American embassy located in downtown Fukuoka. It was March 17, 1952, two years to the day since James first professed his love to Tami.

By the time Colonel Palmer came out from his office, the reception area was vacant, and he felt a pang of guilt knowing he had yet another irreversible obstacle to stop their marriage. The next day, March 18, by an act of Congress, the International Marriage Grant was to be terminated, and the colonel was certain James and Miss Tami would never be able to eradicate in time colonel Parmer has imposed latest obtrusion they were unaware of.

Drive through congested downtown thoroughfare of Fukuoka, one must have the skill of a race car driver and more importantly, must have a calmed nerve to be able to maneuver among military vehicles large and small, taxis, rickshaws, bicycles, and jaywalkers. Finally James and Miss Tami were in sight of the embassy, but there was no available parking space nearby or even l blocks away. So James made the spur of a moment decision to double-park the jeep right in front of the embassy, which would be closed in twenty minutes. He jumped out of the jeep, grasping Miss Tami's hand securely and held the marriage documents two years in making dashed inside.

Quickly glanced over the directory on the wall at the entrance, and ran up the stairs into the office of the Foreign Service, he handed the thick manila envelope containing their marriage documents to a clerk sitting at the front desk. The clerk examined each page carefully, not saying a word until he came to Tami's police report which was written in Japanese.

"What's this?" he asked, tapping his finger on the sheet of paper.

"This is the police report from my village police chief, sir," Miss Tami informed, trying to be calm but she sensed something was terribly wrong.

"This report was supposed to be translated in English and be submitted along with the original written in Japanese; it was stated in the letter you received." The clerk said as a matter of fact.

"Sir, I was directed, in no uncertain terms, the police report must be written in Japanese. I never received the letter you've just mentioned," James protested. Tami was ill with the prospect of an irreversible error and she was unable to stop her tears.

"By the way, Lieutenant, tomorrow is March the eighteenth, and at 4:30 p.m. all international marriages will be denied, and all documents will be inadvisable," the clerk informed James.

Miss Tami's blood drained from her brain, and she was in a near faint, and James was in shock, but quickly regaining his composure he became furious.

"If what you've just said is true, then tell me this, when would the permission be granted again?" James asked, trying hard to be civil.

"I don't know for sure, but usually in about two years the Congress will re-enact section 72, title 22 of the United States Code." the clerk said as a matter of fact.

Overwhelmed with the unexpected bad news, Miss Tami and James walked out of the embassy in a daze.

"James, take me to the train station. I'm going to get that report and be back in time for us to get married." Tami shouted, and she remembered something very important. *"Oh, James, I have very exciting news, I meant to tell you since this morning."* She then told him about the package that had been delivered from the United States, and she knew instantly the contents were their rings.

"Our rings has arrived this morning." she said elatedly, although her voice carried a tone of conflicting irony.

"That's wonderful, darling. Have you looked at them?" James asked happily, trying to cheer her up.

"No, I didn't. I thought we'd open it together and make our engagement official by putting the rings on each other's finger," Tami said somberly.

Arrived at the train station, in time for Tami to catch the next scheduled run and before boarding, Miss Tami quickly wrote a note explaining her reason for not coming home tonight, asked James to deliver it to me.

The train stopped at every station, and would take four hours instead of the usual hour and a half by express; it would be dark when she arrived at her destination. Feeling vulnerable, Miss Tami has imagined James was sitting next to her and said, *"Remember, I am with you every step of the way. Return safely. I'll be right here waiting when you return."* Miss Tami has hung onto the sound of James's voice and the words he said to her before she left.

By the time Miss Tami reached her destination night had fallen and few people disembarked quickly from the train disappeared into the night. Miss Tami looked for a taxi but there was none, and all those little stores lining each side of the street were standing in eerie mute darkness. Alone in a pitch-dark moonless night, Miss Tami had no other choice but to start walking, watching the ground in front of her to avoid potholes and protruding rocks.

"I should be home by midnight." She said out loud, without looking into the infinite looming darkness.

Suddenly a beam of bright light shot Miss Tami from behind startled her. Looking over her shoulder, Miss Tami saw the headlights a taxi, slowing down for her. Normally this taxi would have been at the train station, but tonight the driver could not get the engine started; but finally got the engine running, and he drove straight to the station, but the place was deserted. *"I've got here too late, no one's there. I'd best go home,"* Shohei, the driver, said to himself, and he turned around to head back home. But an unexplainable sensation came over Shohei, and he felt compelled to turn and drive in the opposite direction. And he had not gone very far before he recognized Miss Tami walking alone on the side of the road, stopped to offer her a ride.

"I was so frightened. I am glad you came." Tami said, after she was safely inside the taxi.

"I had no idea anyone was walking at this time of the night, especially you, Miss Araki; it's dangerous at night even for a man. I can't think of any other reason than the loving spirits must've been guarding you," Shohei said solemnly.

It was after midnight when Miss Tami reached the estate. Shohei escorted her to the house. Hearing the approaching footsteps, Tenshi began barking frantically woke the servants. They came out holding clubs and knives in their hands to apprehend the late-night intruder, but Tenshi's frantic bark changed to a whimper and then he began yelping.

"It is I, your mistress, and this is the taxi driver Shohei, who brought me here." Miss Tami spoke, while trying to calm an excited Tenshi.

Yumi came running, jolted out of a sound sleep. Miss Tami apologized for her unannounced late-night arrival, assuring everyone she would explain in the morning, and then she asked Shohei to be back for her at eight the following morning. Briefly Miss Tami explained the reason for her sudden return to Yumi, and informed the servants she will explain everything in a morning.

Tearfully acknowledging the news, Yumi wished her mistress and Lieutenant Courtland all the happiness for their union. In a morning, she has prepared a morning bath and a traditional morning meal for her mistress.

Shohei arrived precisely at 8:00AM. And Miss Tami bid her final farewell to all, and to Tenshi he has sensed his mistress was not coming back; he began to whimper and followed her, ignoring her *"Stay"* command. Miss Tami knelt in front of Tenshi, stroking him gently and speaking to him as if he was her child.

"My faithful Tenshi, I know you are saddened to see me go, but we must part, for I am going to be with my husband, whom I love very much, and you must guard the people you and I care very much. Having you here I feel secure. I love you my faithful friend." Miss Tami said, hugging Tenshi, then she waved good-bye to the tear-blurred figures in the background and walked away into the waiting taxi.

Miss Tami had Shohei drove to the village police station, but the police chief was not in, so she waited in the taxi. Half an hour has passed but still no chief; even after an hour had passed there was any sign of the police chief, and time was getting short. Feeling upset, Miss Tami used the police station phone to call the chief, informing him that he had an urgent matter at hand. Luckily the police station had the only telephone in the village.

The chief was not pleased, having to forego his usual leisurely morning routine of having breakfast and taking his time to read the newspaper, but he was needed for a rare urgent matter, and the cab would be there to pick him up. The police chief gave Miss Tami his full cooperation; he even located an old Remington typewriter, in a storage room, which never has been used before because no one had the enough knowledge of English to type.

Miss Tami has volunteered to type while the chief dictated, the report was quickly updated and signed, but the name of the translator had to be someone other than Miss Tami.

A young rookie, fresh out of high school, was chosen because he knows English, but he confessed that he knew only a few words of English he learned in high school. *"I've learned very little English. It was hard, and no one passed the test; I made it with a D."* he said trying to hide an embarrassment, thus standing at attention as if he was nailed to the floor.

"At ease, officer. I thank you for willing to help me." Miss Tami said to the tremulous young man, watched the color come back on his face; and he smiled being addressed as an officer. Also to be the translator, he needed some coaxing because he was fearful of the responsibility.

Miss Tami informed the police chief; the letter was already typed and needs only his signature, along with his rank and title.

Eventually the deed was done, and Miss Tami hoped her small deception would not be discovered.

Miss Tami thanked the chief and the rookie for their help, she left the village police station, hurried into the taxi, and Shohei raced to the train depot while Miss Tami was nervously calculating the timing of her schedule. She must not miss the 1:30 express back to the city, to be at her destination by 3:00 p.m., which would give her and James thirty minutes to make it to the embassy on time.

After she purchased a train ticket, Miss Tami gave all the money she had in her purse to Shohei and thanked him repeatedly for his help. Shohei was aghast to see the amount of money Miss Tami placed in his hand, and then Miss Tami removed the Longine watch from her wrist, put it in his hand and fold his fingers over the watch *"For your wife,"* she said with a smile. And then Miss Tami ran to board the train before Shohei could thank her.

Miss Tami felt the train was slowly gaining speed; and Shohei was standing on the platform watching through tear-bleared eyes, and disappeared out of sight.

"Why the sad tears? I should be happy for her." Shohei said to himself, but he was unable to stop his welling tears.

Miss Tami knew James was waiting, at the train station, for her arrival since the morning, but Miss Tami was not on each arriving train. And

"She has got to be on the next one." Miss Tami visualized James waiting desperately for me to be on the train, as James waited and watched the disembarking passengers. Then at 3:30 p.m. Tami walked off the train looking pale and exhausted from the two days of ordeals, but her anxiety vanished as James embraced her in a warm hug, and his kisses made her feel warm all over.

"We must hurry, dear." James urged, and together they ran out from the train station, climbed into the jeep, headed for the embassy as James maneuvered the jeep in and out of the congested traffics. Tami read the police chief's statement once more to spot errors if any. Please, nothing must go wrong, she prayed. As they approached closer to the embassy, again there was no parking space available, just as same as yesterday.

At that instant James double-parked in front of the embassy again and jumped out of the jeep, grabbed hold of Miss Tami's hand, and together they dashed in through the door and ran up the stairs two at a time into the office of Foreign Affairs, where the same clerk was sitting at the desk.

Again James handed the manila envelope to him that has contained their marriage documents of two years in the making, and this time he laid the same manila envelope containing the letter written by the police chief.

The clerk was startled to see the officer and a girl suddenly appeared in a front of him, and it took him a moment to realize they had been there yesterday. He picked up the envelope, removed the letter and read it, thoroughly inspected the contents of letter. Tami gripped James's hand and waited for the clerk to say something, fearing he would detect her deception; surely the clerk would hear her loud pounding heart.

Finally he looked up from the letter and gave a nod, a sign of approval. At that moment, both James and Tami felt their knees weaken from relief. They watched the clerk produce the marriage license from his desk drawer; he summoned the office girl and had James and Tami's names typed in, wrote his signature, and embossed it with the seal of the American embassy. He then asked James and Tami to raise their right hand. At that moment two office girls joined them as the witnesses to their marriage ceremony.

"You, sir, Lieutenant James Thomas Courtland, are you legally free to be married to Miss Tami Araki?"

"Yes." James answered.

Then clerk turned to Tami.

"Miss Tami Araki, are you legally free to be married to Lieutenant James Thomas Courtland?" Miss Tami answered yes, with her wobbly voice, holding her tears back.

"You two are now legally married husband and wife, Congratulations." the clerk pronounced, and at that moment two years of agonizing trials and tribulations suddenly vanished. James and Tami were now Lieutenant and Mrs. Courtland, and the time was exactly 4:30 p.m., March 18, 1952.

James and Tami headed toward the embassy exit hand in hand, jubilant as they could possibly be. Just then a GI and a young girl came bursting in through the door and ran up the stairs to the same office James and Tami had been, but the door was closed. The man began to knock on the door, and then pounded with his fist to no avail; the door remained locked. Having arrived a moment too late, the groom- and bride-to-be were denied the right to marriage. Now they would have to wait two more years or perhaps even longer, for the U.S. Congress to reenact section 72 titles 22 of the United States Code, and then they would have to restart the procedure all over again. The young girl began to sob, and her fiancé was unable to console her. As Tami looked on, she realized the sad scene she and James had just witnessed could have been theirs.

"I must go home to see Taka; she must be worried sick. Oh, the rings—I haven't seen them; I wanted us to open it together." Tami said, looking up admiringly at her new husband. Arriving at the apartment, I was told the news of their marriage; I felt solemn but expressed my congratulatory wishes.

"Tami, the rings. Let us see the rings," James asked excitedly.

Miss Tami ran to her bedroom and brought out the cardboard box, still sealed with postal tape. Using his key James slit the postal tape; ripped open the box, put his hand through the packing materials, and brought out a smaller box, which contained two black velvet ring cases. James handed one to Miss Tami, and he opened the other. Miss Tami's case had the wedding rings and James's had the engagement rings. The flawless diamonds had become even more brilliant now that they were set between the classic purple amethysts on the eighteen-karat-gold engagement ring.

"The rings are so beautiful. I am pleased." Miss Tami said, unable to take her eyes off the sparkling symbol of their love.

"It truly is a beautiful ring, befitting to our love for each other. I am overwhelmed. I have no word to express how I feel, except to tell you that I love you." James said, putting the engagement ring on Tami's finger, held her hand looked into her eyes, and he asked, "Miss Tami, will you please marry me?"

"Yes, I will marry you, Lieutenant Courtland." Tami said, looking up into his sparkling blue eyes. *"We are now officially engaged, and married."* she said and placed the wedding bands on each other's finger, and then Tami took his left hand wearing the wedding ring, placed it over her heart and said, *"I love you, my husband. I'll love you forever."*

The newlyweds planned to spend their first night together at the apartment, and while Taka was preparing dinner, James went back to his quarters to pick up the rest of his belongings.

Tami was nervous as she prepared to share her bed with a man for the first time, even though he was her husband whom she loved more than her own life. Moreover, Tami had dreamt and fantasized about making passionate love with James; however, tonight was not a fantasy, and Tami feared that her lack of experience would disappoint him. Sensing Tami's disquietude, I have suggested she have a relaxing bath, and drew a warm bath for the new bride. Also time has come to present Miss Tami with the small atomizer contained the rare orchid perfume, I have been waiting ever since Mistress Shizuka said, *"I know when the right time to give to Miss Tami."* saving for so many years.

"Miss Tami, this rare scent was a special gift from your father to your mother," I have explained. *"Your mother has requested me to safeguard it for you until the time was right for you to have it."* And she added just a few drops of the perfume to Tami's bathwater, an instantly the sweet aroma of exotic orchids filled the air.

Lying in the scented bath, Tami's tense body began to relax, and she closed her eyes and stretched in the warm water.

She felt the touch of a soft washcloth tenderly caressing her shoulder, moving down to her arm. Tami, in her dreamy moment, imagined y I bathed her as a child, then in an instant her illusion vanished, and to her surprise James was kneeling at the side of bathtub, his sleeves rolled up, with a washcloth in his hand. *"James, please—you can't be in here."* Tami cried out, trying to cover herself, but there was only the water to hide under.

"Don't be shy, my darling bride. Remember? I'm your husband who loves you; nothing's wrong with being naked in front of me," James assured her. This was Tami's first encounter as a wife, and she soon learned that all the rest would follow naturally. When she stepped out of the bath, James helped her with her robe and dried her hair.

I have prepared a special dinner for their wedding night, serving perfectly broiled steaks and my own sauce with a touch of ginger. Also I placed on the table, was a centerpiece of red and white roses. James complimented me for the cooking skill I learned in just a short period, and conveyed his special appreciation since he and Miss Tami have not had decent meals of late.

Newlywed couple was sitting on the sofa, relaxing and listening to soft music as they sipped after-dinner brandy. Miss Tami rested her head on James's chest, feeling the pulsating rhythm of his heartbeat. Soon she began to fall asleep holding an empty wineglass, that was almost fell from her hand.

Carefully James removed the wineglass, scooped Miss Tami up, and carried his sleepy bride into the bedroom, where he laid her on the already turned down perfumed bed and disrobed her. And then quickly removed his clothes and gotten into the bed next to his bride.

James was marveling at her cherry red lips and flawless blushed pink complexion, James began kissing Tami softly. Miss Tami, for the first time seduced by a magic of love and sweet brandy, moaned and her body moved with an uncontrollable throbbing pleasure, as James's lips caressed her firm breasts and smooth abdomen, and his tongue devoured its way to her thighs. Slowly and gently James parted the tender petals. Miss Tami was on fire; she clawed at anything in her reach, drowning in the heat of erotic passion, and then she felt James's rigid manhood slowly penetrate her blossoming womanhood.

Miss Tami felt a pain of first consummation, but smothered by a passion of red-hot fire, Miss Tami's seal of virgin has resisted James; as it heightened his pleasure of orgasm yet more he kept whispering, *"Ohhh, my love, I love you."* pushing his rigid shaft deeper into her as his motions became rapid and James exploded, and they for the first time experienced the heights of orgasm.

Miss Tami and James lay limp in each other's arms as their fast-beating hearts began to calm. James gathered Tami's soft body against his and used his fingertip to push her perspiration-dampened hair away from her face. Tami was reborn that moment through the pain of nuptial consummation, and she emerged as a whole woman. Her young body healed quickly, as they became the perfectly matched couple.

Chapter 12: World Afar

A year after they were married James completed his tour of duty and began the process to leave Japan, and Miss Tami has retained a lawyer and transferred all her assets to me and Yumi, stipulating her five servants were to be provided with enough income to enable them to live comfortably. She also set aside a trust fund for Shohei, the taxi driver, and his wife to live comfortably for the rest of their lives.

After resigning as Colonel Palmer's secretary, Miss Tami vacated her apartment, and she and James stayed at a hotel until the day of their departure. Miss Tami knew she must dismiss me, a profoundly difficult task which she delayed as long as possible, but finally the time came when delaying was no longer possible, and Miss Tami informed me that she must return to the estate.

Although Miss Tami and I have known, someday she and I must to part and have to go a separate way, follow the path of destiny. But an inevitable day of parting was knocking our door; hit Miss Tami hard; she was unable to contain herself, and first time she cried openly in front of me. Miss Tami has managed to hold on to her composure and explained briefly about Yumi and me of rights to the estate, along with all of Miss Tami's belongings.

On the eve of departure, James, Miss Tami, and I have shared a final meal together, at the hotel restaurant. Soon after the table was cleared, Miss Tami held my hands firmly in her hand, expressed sincere gratitude for a lifetime of selfless devotion.

She then handed a large brown envelope containing documents. *"This is for you and your sister Yumi,"* Tami said. And leaving all I own to both you and Yumi, so neither of you will ever have to suffer hardship again. Also, there are five envelopes containing documents for my servants and a separate envelope for Shohei, so he and his wife may live in comfort and dignity.

"All my life, you have been the mother to me in many regards; however, you and I have come to a moment in our lives when we must go our separate ways. You and Yumi will meet a nice man and marry, and you will have families, just as I will with my husband James. Go in good health, and be happy." Miss Tami has managed to convey her heartfelt farewell to me, her loving surrogate mother, without losing composure, but her voice could no longer pass through the big lump in her throat, and she was unable to continue.

The next morning the movers came, packed all of Miss Tami and my belongings, and drove away to the estate. I saw Miss Tami and Lieutenant from smoked rear window of the limousine, until disappeared among the traffic. At that moment Tami buried her face against James's chest, broke down and cried as if her heart was ripping apart. Even James's tender hugs could not ease her pain.

In August 1953, James and Tami left Japan. James was looking forward to his homecoming, but Tami was moving to an unknown new world.

The day of James and Tami's arrival, James's twin brother

Thomas was at LAX, much earlier than their flight's scheduled landing; he simply could not sit at home and watch the slowly moving hands of his watch. It was three years ago James was shipped off to Japan, and the long-awaited day of his return was finally here, but James was bringing his new wife, a Japanese girl.

Thomas could not shake off his apprehension about James's wife Tami, because there had been so many news reports about Japanese wives being abandoned by their ex-GI husbands. The GI left his home, family, and girlfriend to answer the call of duty, fell in love when he was alone and far from home, but when he returned home he no longer needed his Japanese wife and children to fill his void. But Thomas knew his brother James was a kind and considerate man; he would never abandon his wife.

Finally there was an announcement, of James and his wife's flight's arrival Thomas heard to the gate, and shortly the disembarking passengers began to come through the corridor. Thomas had his eyes glued to the people, and then he saw James. His brother looked a little older and taller than he remembered, because he was much leaner than when he went overseas; his face was tanned from being outdoors as a soldier on duty.

"Jimmy!" Thomas shouted, frantically waving his arms. James saw him and broke out in a big smile, sidestepping a group of people, holding a beautiful Oriental girl's hand.

Nearly crashing into each other, the brothers hugged, shook hands, and hugged some more, and then James introduced his wife, Miss Tami to Thomas. He was awestruck standing in front of an astonishingly beautiful woman, tried to greet her as a respectable brother-in-law should, but his words came out as an embarrassing stutter. Miss Tami was just as astounded to see the two identical men; the only difference was Thomas had a slight southern accent.

"I am very happy to meet you; James told me so much about you." Was all Tami could manage, and she bowed to her brother-in-law.

As they drove through the city of Los Angeles, Miss Tami could not believe her eyes. The scene was nothing like the narrow and congested streets so full of people in Japan; here was a view of huge expanse of cityscape, and the wide freeways look s if a monstrous spider web took Tami's breathes away.

Arrived at Thomas's apartment in downtown Los Angeles and settled in the best they could, but the bachelor's apartment was too small for three people, so James and Miss Tami began apartment hunting. Even more urgently, they needed a car, which James has not considered until now. For three years he had a military jeep at his disposal, and the realization that he was a civilian without the privileges of USAF lieutenant. He needed a car to go shopping for a vehicle. Borrowed Thomas's car, and went apartment hunting.

Miss Tami walked right into a world which she knew nothing, and world she knew has turned upside down. And more often than not she embarrassed herself, caught between the casual Americans' open, friendly lifestyle. Until now Miss Tami has considered herself as a sophisticated and culturally educated individual, but the ceremonial rituals she was used to performing when introduced to someone new were no longer appropriate; inadvertently she found herself in several embarrassing situations.

"This is my wife Tami," James would say as he introduced this extraordinarily beautiful Oriental girl to his acquaintances. And he has immensely enjoyed seeing his friends staring at Tami wide-eyed.

Miss Tami, as a courtesy to James's friend, and being a respectable wife, performed her ritual of proper speech making and bowed deeply to the person she was met for a first time. However, James had to tell her there was no need for bowing or a befitting speech; he was trying not to embarrass Tami. *"All you have to do is say, 'Very nice to meet you."* That has answered Miss Tami's puzzlement about why the people acted so uneasy.

"I've made a fool of myself; I'm sorry, James. I was being courteous so your friends will respect you more, but instead I've embarrassed you." Miss Tami apologized, trying not to show her teary eyes.

"Tami, my love, you did not embarrass me. You have no idea how proud I am of you, and most of all I love you for what you are, my lovely bride." James whispered as he held her close and kissed her cheek.

Miss Tami has learn about the American culture each step of the way, and more importantly, to be Mrs. James Courtland she had to learn to be a housewife, which she had no experience because the servants had always been there to meet her every need. Luckily Miss Tami can read instruction manuals, recipes, and ask questions. Still she was caught in between the overwhelming cultural differences that have existed between the two countries, and she did not know how to fit in. Miss Tami recalled a passage from a book she read long ago: East is east, and West is west, and never the twain shall meet. This puzzling thought hung in her mind all these years, but she never understood until now. Her mind began to unravel the mystery hidden behind the words, as she recognized herself in new environs Tami and I had promised each other to keep in touch, and they wrote letters often. As always Tami began with. You could never imagine? or I went to the supermarket, and you would never believe the size of … and then always ended her letter with, I miss all of you so much.

Thirty days had passed since James and Miss Tami arrived in the United States; and James had to be formally discharged from the Air Force, which nearest base was the San Diego Naval Base, and he and Miss Tami drove down to the San Diego Naval Base, while Miss Tami witnessed her husband, Lieutenant James courtland has officially became a civilian again.

Soon after James was discharged, he and Thomas formed a partnership in the advertising business, and with increased manpower the business grew so much so that in just one year, it became necessary to obtain more befitting larger office.

The real estate agency was contacted to locate an elegant and spacious office, preferably in a prestigious new high-rise business complex, and they named the new firm T. and J. Advertising Agency. It was Miss Tami's idea to use the first initial of James Thomas. Since then the business prospered and acquired many more new clients, both large and small businesses. Thomas and James hired a competent all-female team of office personnel, also Tami's idea, and those women must be sophisticated, attractive, and have a degree in business management; they also had to win Miss Tami's approval to be hired.

For the next five years, the partnership continued to prosper, and together Thomas and James purchased a beautiful white house, atop a Santa Monica hillside with a view of the Pacific Ocean. James and Miss Tami resided in the main white house, with the interior done in a classic eggshell white, accented with a natural hardwood floor throughout the five-thousand-square-foot two-story home. Just inside the wide front entrance, there was a winding staircase to the upstairs Miss Tami loved her new house, and there was a room adjoining the kitchen with a floor-to-ceiling sliding glass door facing the Pacific Ocean. Every evening before the sun set, it was ritual to sit and watched a huge orange sun melt down behind the earth's curvature line. Miss Tami and James sat on a soft tan-colored leather sofa, sipping fragrant hot green tea as they watched *"Taka must be up by now and having a morning hot tea,"* Tami thought out loud. James knew what was on her mind, and hugged her softly.

Thomas lived in the guesthouse, behind main resident quota which had a floor-to-ceiling sliding glass door in view the Pacific Ocean; sitting on a high back rattan chair shaded by massive blazing red bougainvillea climbed an arbor, an extending patio deck casting shade on the patio vivid contrast against the white guesthouse. Thomas liked to sit on the patio and watch the ocean; he often caught sight of a whale.

James and Miss Tami spoke of having a child, but an each month passed in disappointment, so to take their minds off the matter, they often went on weekend getaways headed north to Big Sur, telling Thomas, *" Be back Sunday night."* One such weekend they left as usual saying, "We'll be back ..."

"Have a good time; I'll be here when you come back." Thomas said to them, and he was thinking of which restaurant to go to for some special cuisine, because he did not like to dine alone. Afterwards I'll have a drink at a bar in Beverly Hills, he thought, planning to go to a place many of his business acquaintances frequented. And *"Tomorrow, I'll check out Venice Beach, where the action is."*

Few hours after Miss Tame and James left there was knocking at the front door. Who could that be? Thomas thought and opened the door, and he saw two state police officers.

"Sir, do you have a brother named James and his wife—ah, ah, she's an Oriental?" An officer asked, unable to pronounce Tami's name.

"Yes, I do. What's wrong, Officer? Did something happen to them?" Thomas spurted out desperately frightened, and then, one of the officers informed him with a regret, that James and

Miss Tami had been in an auto accident. Apparently they met an oncoming car driven by a drunk driver.

Judging from skid mark on pavement, James has attempted to avoid the head-on collision, but their car veered off the road and fell to the rocky beach below, killing him instantly. Miraculously Miss Tami had survived, but she suffered a concussion and multiple fractures. Immediately she was taken to the local hospital emergency room, and James's body to the hospital morgue.

Unable to grasp the full impact of this sudden horrific news, Thomas's mind spiraled down into a black vacuum; however, the law required him to identify the body, and the officers drove him to the hospital. Viewing the body, Thomas acknowledged indeed it was James, his twin brother, and then accompanied by a nurse Thomas went to see Miss Tami in the intensive care unit.

Standing outside of the curtain, Thomas listened for any sound from Tami, but he heard only beeping sounds, and saw a light shadow being cast on the curtain. Thomas parted the curtain with his finger, just enough to see Tami lying on a bed, and he saw the tubes inserted in Tami's mouth and nose.

There was a black cuff on her arm and an IV in the back of one hand, and the monitor was showing Tami's vital signs. Thomas stared for a while at the irregular red line as it ran across the screen. He knew this was Tami lying in the bed, but she was unrecognizable. Thomas was horrified. Her face was bruised, swollen to the size of a small watermelon, and her eyes were swollen shut. The only familiar thing about her was her hair, which had been brushed and braided carefully and lay beside her on the pillow. Thomas walked closer. *Tami— it's Thomas, can you hear me?"* He said, and brought his face close to her, looking for a sign of response.

"She can't hear you." A voice came from behind. It was the

intensive care nurse. *"She's comatose, sir,"* the nurse informed him. The two police officers stood in the background quietly observing the goings-on.

"Will she come out of it anytime soon?" Thomas asked, alarmed by Tami's appearance but the nurse did not answer his question; she only informed him that the doctor was waiting in his office to talk to him.

According to the doctor, it was a miracle that Tami had survived the crash that killed her husband instantly; however, she was in critical condition and must remain in intensive care. Thomas would be informed immediately if there were any changes. The doctor then handed Thomas a large envelope containing James and Tami's personal effects.

Thomas opened it and checked the contents. He was overwhelmed by a strange sadness at seeing the familiar wallet, wedding and engagement rings, and Tami's purse, which had been in her possession when he saw those just hours earlier. Especially the custom-made engagement rings Thomas saw on their fingers. *"Please, this isn't happening."* Thomas said to himself unable to accept the sudden turn of tragedy.

For the next three months, Thomas was in constant contact with the doctor, but the answer was always the same, *"No change in her condition."*

One day, a call came from the doctor; it was the news Thomas had been waiting for.

"She is awake!" The doctor said excitedly.

Before heading out to the hospital, Thomas picked out some of Tami's clothes for her to wear, acceptation of maybe Miss Tami could come home, and he also gathered up few of her toiletries, but Thomas's kind gesture was turned out to be a grave mistake. Entering the hospital, Thomas immediately went into the doctor's office, but the doctor had a serious expression on his face. Thomas knew instantly something was wrong.

"*Mr. Courtland,*" the doctor began. "Your sister-in-law has been removed from the ICU, and she is resting comfortably in a private room."

When Thomas heard the doctor, his expectation of taking Miss Tami home has vanished. "*However,*" the doctor continued, "*I must inform you that she is suffering from amnesia. She does not remember anything, even her own name, except she has been asking for James. I have not told her of James's passing, for fear she would not understand, but seeing you she may respond differently.*" The doctor sounded hopeful.

In a spacious and airy private room with a view of the Pacific Ocean, Tami was lying in a larger and more comfortable bed without the IV and wires. Tami's swelling and massive bruises were almost gone, and the fullness of her face had wasted away from loss of weight. She appeared to be asleep. Walking up to her bed, Thomas laid his hand very lightly on her arm and stared into her thin face while the doctor kept his vigil from the opposite side of the bed.

"*Tami, Tami dear—it's Thomas. Can you hear me?*" Thomas whispered. Miss Tami stirred and opened her eyes, trying to focus on the person who spoke, then for a millisecond, a sign of recognition appeared in her eyes, but it faded quickly.

"*I thought you were James,*" she said and closed her eyes.

Even though Thomas tried to carry on a conversation, she would not respond; and then the doctor motioned him to follow him out the room.

"*You must remember, Mr. Courtland, Tami does not know you; however, she showed an encouraging sign. As soon as she is physically well enough, we can transfer her to the hospital closer to you in Los Angeles.*" The doctor was optimistic.

For the first time since the accident, Thomas left the hospital feeling elated. He left Miss Tami's clothes and shoes with her attending nurse. At last, Thomas thought as he regained his hope of bringing Miss Tami home, where she would be in familiar surroundings, which would surely bring her memory back.

But no sooner had Thomas begun to think the worst was over an urgent call from the doctor informing Miss Tami's disappearance. This newest turn struck Thomas like a bolt of lightning.

The thorough search was on, in and out, all around the hospital compound to find Tami, but she was nowhere to be seen. Tami must have found her clothes, put them on, and simply walked out of the building.

An all-points bulletin was out on Tami. It described her to the smallest detail, with the added caution that she was not a suspect but a missing hospital patient who was suffering amnesia and in need of medical attention. In the coming days, Thomas created flyers and posted them around the hospital and in places he thought Tami might have gone. But despite the thorough search, there was no sign of Miss Tami.

Two years went by, and in spite of Miss Tami's striking appearance, no one has seen her. Then one day the corpse of an Oriental female was found in an alley of the Little Tokyo. The frail body appeared so emaciated it, the woman must have starved to death. A detective visited Thomas to break the news and ask him to identify the body. The corpse was skin and bone, but Thomas could tell it was definitely Miss Tami, so he thought...

The past two years of Miss Tami's life were in no way traceable, not even to Miss Tami herself. Thomas could only surmise she was searching for James, lost in her confused world.

Thomas had lost track of passing time; sitting on rattan chair, thinking about sudden upheaval of his routine everyday life, inconceivable that his brother James is gone, and Miss Tami's were about is unknown, and the pain of losing both Miss Tami and James was unbearable.

"*Uncle Tommy.*" Thomas heard a voice of a small child calling his name, and he turning around to see who was calling him. That when Thomas saw apparition of James, but not Miss Tami.

James was standing behind him, and he was holding a child about two years old, who had long shiny auburn hair just like Miss Tami's, and then James said something to a child and put her down.

"*Uncle Tommy...*" The little girl said and came running with unsteady toddler's feet, jumped into Thomas's open arms, hugged his neck and pressed her soft cheek on his. It was an astonishing moment to see those images of James and the precious little Nisei child. However, the Miss Tami was not with them?

Thomas had a glimpse into their world; although the images soon vanished but etched in his mind as clear as day, and an assurance of they were with me, and I am not alone; enable him to go on with his life.

Since then, Thomas has often heard the sweet voice of a child calling, "*Uncle Tommy.*" He turned around to see his little niece standing there, realizing it was a figment of his imagination, but for a moment the illusory images of loved ones warmed his heart.

Every evening as usual, Thomas sat on a white leather sofa in the living room, gazing at a huge orange ball melting slowly down below the horizon on the edge of the Pacific Ocean watching the sunset Tami has never missed. *"It's an early morning in Japan. The servants must all be up by now getting ready for their daily chores, and Taka is having a hot cup of tea."* Miss Tami has often said wistfully, as if she could actually see the estate and its people.

The night had long been fallen, and the massive silver moonbeams dancing on the ocean waves reflecting off the large portrait of James and Miss Tami hanging over the mantel. Thomas stared at the moonlit ocean as his mind retraced that incomprehensible fatal chain of events, knowing he would have to live with the inexplicable pain for the rest of his life.

"I must notify Taka and Yumi immediately." Thomas thought; and he is well aware that his letter would inflict pain and sadness on them for as long as they live. I will write to them tomorrow, trying to find a way not to hurt them, but there was no other way of cushioning their pain.

Chapter 13: Taka

Every day I waited for the postman to bring a letter from Miss Tami, thinking maybe today? As my anxious mind hoped, but weeks and months have passed without a word from her; and I was sick with worry, even though I told myself no news is good news. But thought did not give me the relief I sought, so I wrote more letters to her and waited.

Then one day a package arrived from the United States. Finally! I thought, but an odd sensation arose in my mind, a package? I questioned myself, even though I could not read the address label, I knew the package was not from Miss Tami. I opened it and there was an envelope resting on top of the contents, and the letter was written in English, which told me something was very wrong. I began to shake. *"Yumi, come quickly. Now!"* I shouted. Hearing my frantic voice, Yumi came running. I handed her the letter saying, *"It's not from Miss Tami."* Yumi said and sensed ill karma as I did, and her face turned white as a sheet of paper. She sat down as if she had been dropped, with the letter in her hand,

and both of us realized whatever was written in this letter was not good news. My heart began to beat rapidly.

Suddenly Tenshi came running; he must have sensed Miss Tami's scent, and he put his nose in the box, sniffing the contents as if searching for something, and then he looked directly at me as if asking, *"Where is my master?"* I stroked his head and spoke to him. *"Tenshi dear, something is very wrong; but I can't bring myself to say the words."* Tenshi did not budge, waiting for me to say something more, but I had no words to ease his anxiety.

Immediately I summoned Shohei, take me to the police station, explaining,

"I must see the officer who can read the English." He was the one who helped Miss Tami with a letter the police chief wrote for her, and she addressed him as an officer even though he was only a rookie. Entering the police station, I walked over to his desk and handed him the letter I had in my hand, asking him to translate it for me. The young police officer noticed the letter was written in English and brought out his dictionary. I sat down next to him at his desk as he began to read the letter, and in a few moments his face froze and he was unable to continue. *"What is it? What does it say?"* I asked nervously.

"Ma'am, this letter is from Mr. Thomas Courtland," he said solemnly. I knew that Thomas Courtland was Lieutenant Courtland's twin brother. *"I will do my best to translate as written."* After he regained his composure he began.

Dear Ms. Taka and Ms. Yumi:

I regret having to inform you that my brother James has passed away. He was killed instantly in an auto accident, and Tami was critically injured and unconscious, hospitalized in the intensive care unit. She was comatose but awoke after three months, and she had amnesia and lost all her memories, even of herself, although, miraculously, she remembered her husband James. Then one day Tami was discovered missing; apparently she walked out of the hospital unnoticed. I searched for her by putting ads in the local newspaper and passing out flyers with her picture on them at the restaurants and shops where Tami and James frequented. Then I received a call from the detective whom I had hired to find her, and he informed me that a female corpse was found and could be Tami, and the body was taken to the L.A. Charity Hospital morgue. I prayed it was not Tami. The corpse I viewed was unrecognizably thin, far from Tami as I remembered, but it was not Tami, and she is missing a missing person police are looking for her. All this time I have kept the house just as she left it, so after Tami was found, I could bring her home to her familiar surroundings, hoping help Tami to regain her memory. It is inconceivable that I lost my only family. I do sincerely express my heartfelt condolence to you, Miss Taka and Miss Yumi.

Thomas

Calmly I have informed Shohei the sad news, and I heard him make a choking sound; afterwards he drove in silence. I am painfully regretting not being at Miss Tami's side when she needed me the most; if I had been there, Miss Tami would not have wandered away from the hospital, I would care for her even if she did not recognize me.

The servants took the news of Miss Tami's missing with sad hearts, and they planted a pink peach tree in her memory, next to her parents and grandfather. Tenshi slept most of the day lying next to the peach tree; he had aged just as we had, and he is no longer an active dog.

One day Ohi found him dead lying under the peach tree, and the loss of Tenshi has devastated Ohi, he was inconsolable heartbroken man, unable to accept the deaths of both his beloved

Tenshi and Miss Tami. Ken engraved a likeness of Tenshi on a matching black marble slab and placed it where the peach tree will always cast its shade over Tenshi's resting place while Miss Tami sitting next him.

Yumi married Ken, and they became the proud parents of a baby girl named Tamiko. They built their house with the nursery attached right next to mine. Strangely my niece Tamiko resembles Miss Tami, but perhaps it's my imagination.

Ken was a quiet man, who did not talk much before he and Yumi were married, but now he talks nonstop about their baby Tamiko; finally, he was able to put whatever haunted him from his prior life behind him. Every afternoon, after Tamiko awakes from her nap, Ken and Yumi take her for a walk around the garden in a buggy. Seeing them I weep; it brings back the memory of pushing baby Miss Tami in a buggy around the garden.

Ohi brings gifts of his first-harvested fruit and vegetables, bouquets of flowers, and an exquisite bonsai he made for me. Apparently for the first time in his life he feels wealthy and wants to share his life with me as man and wife, but I want us only to be good friends and companions, caring for each other as we grow old together, because my heart belongs to Tamiko, as I imagine holding an infant Miss Tami in my bosom.

The years have passed as fast as the changing seasons, and my niece Tamiko has grown into a stunningly beautiful young woman. She married her literature professor, and they have two children, a boy and a girl. Shingo is four years old and very protective of his two-year-old sister Yumiko, who resembles Miss Tami with her large dark almond eyes, long shiny black hair with a deep blue hue that sparkles as she moves, and even more, her voice startles me at times, making me think I heard little Miss Tami calling me Nana.

Hiroshi, the ex-kamikaze pilot, returned to the university, resumed his education, and became an airline pilot. He flies internationally as well as domestically. Hiroshi is a very handsome young man, looking especially grand in his pilot's uniform. When he comes to visit with me in between his assigned flights, he never forgets to bring a box of fancy chocolate from a faraway country and a single white rose for Miss Tami. I am hoping he will find a nice girl who will be his wife in the near future.

Taro has opened a factory and hired ten employees. They produce prepared foods with many varieties of sushi, grilled tuna steak, sliced pickles, and fresh vegetables. Not only does Taro cook them, but he also cuts them to resemble flowers, complemented by parsley artfully placed in a package proudly displaying his logo. Taro met a young woman at an open market where he purchases fresh produce, and each time he went to the market she was there asking him if she can be of help. She was knowledgeable about the produce, always helping him to choose the best. Taro began to rely on her expertise and found himself thinking about her constantly, and then he found out that these feelings were mutual, which led to their marriage. After they were married, Taro's new wife, Naomi, confessed that her being at the market was not a coincidence as he might have thought.

Naomi was a middle-aged woman, strong and hardworking. Not only was she was a good cook, but she also managed the business and the home front. Before the war, she was an apprentice chef working in an upscale restaurant, and at the age of thirteen she had mastered the art of creative cooking. Naomi has received marriage proposals in the past, but she was uninterested and lived happily with her family until the war came. She was the only one of her family to survive the war.

Yoshiki was a bachelor, being perfectly content as a gardener.

He shared a cabin with Ohi, and they kept the estate looking like a showplace. After the loss of Tenshi, Yoshiki saw Ohi wiping tears when he thought no one was around, but Yoshiki knew his friend was suffering with the loss of Tenshi, so one day he surprised Ohi with a puppy about one month old. It was a cute little tan-colored mutt, a bundle of energy running and jumping all over the place.

Ohi saw the puppy and immediately ran to pick him up, but the fat little critter was all excited, running around everywhere, while Ohi chased the rambunctious jumping bundle of energy. Ohi was all out of breath when he finally caught the puppy tried not to drop the rambunctious critter, but it wiggled and wagged in his arms while Ohi was trying to cuddle him. The wiggling puppy licked all over Ohi's scrunched face as rapidly as his tongue would work. It was love at first sight, and Ohi named the puppy Tenshi (an angel,) making him the namesake of the Tenshi he had lost. They were inseparable as the little Tenshi became attached to Ohi's ankle, so it seemed, and followed him everywhere.

Ken made a proposal to renovate the estate, and the first thing to be done was to widen the driveway, which was constructed for pedestrians and rickshaws and was not wide enough for an automobile. The adjoining hill would need to be shaved off to gain the width. Ken proposed to hire Mr. Aoki for the renovation, and Mr. Aoki agreed after Ken contacted him with the idea. One day Mr. Aoki arrived with his two grown sons, who were both architectural engineers. He also brought a landscaping artist to revamp the entire grounds. The landscaping artist took photos from many points to aid in planning the garden, and I was asked to sit in at the meeting for an approval, which took place at my house.

How good it was to see Mr. Aoki after so many years, and we reminisced, recalling the times he has helped us in the past so long ago, and again he will be creating the modern Araki estate. Although many of the details were beyond my comprehension, but Mr. Aoki assured me that just as soon as the drawings and illustrations of the new Araki estate were completed, he would bring them to me for approval.

About a month later he returned with the long rolls of papers. Those were the newly designed color illustrations of the estate, which would be transformed from its present state into another world, one that can only be seen in a modern architectural magazine. I was awestruck looking at each drawing, while Mr. Aoki explained the details to me sheet by sheet.

Half of an adjoining hill was removed, and doubled the width of driveway, and also added a wide sidewalk with a banister for walking visitors. And there were post with solar lamps along the sidewalk, which turns on automatically at dusk and go off at dawn. Ultraviolet rays controlled the automatic opening and closing of the gates, at the bottom of the driveway. *"Imagine that!"* I said to myself in awe.

My new house was similar in design to Miss Tami's apartment in the base; the only difference was I have an altar room adjoining my house, a replica of the family shrine, which stood in the center of the garden. The house overlooked the valley below, instead of looking out over the golf course greens; so that I now enjoyed the same view my Mistress Shizuka had to seek her solace. The panoramic view remained unchanged: Cobalt Pacific and pastel blue sky drew a sliver of silvery line of an earth's curvature. The playground for the children was equipped with the latest state-of-the-art equipments, such as a jungle gym, slide, tree house, swings, large sandbox, and a miniature train running around the perimeter of the playground fence.

Lately I have been thinking about the farmer couple, and I

am planning to visit them in the near future. They have aided us in the past and I would like very much to see them again, taking Ohi and Tenshi along. I have so much news to share with the farmer couple for old times' sake, and as a gift, I am taking a few boxes of Taro's pride and joy, his ready-to-eat packaged food. I will also take a stunningly beautiful wedding photo of Miss Tami and Lieutenant James T. Courtland, but it will be a difficult task to inform them of the passing, knowing their hearts will be broken.

Shohei will drive us in his new taxi, which he bought and had shipped from England. Although the cab was secondhand, but it was new to him and Shohei boasts about being very proud of car's origin and fact that he owns it. The shiny black taxi has a roomy interior and provides a smooth ride over unpaved country roads, just as the limousine ride Miss Tami and I experienced so long ago.

Mr. Ohara has bought the large parcel of property in Fukuoka where black market stalls once lined the street, and he built a huge antique shop simulating a Buddhist shrine. In addition, an elegant teahouse was built to serve complimentary hot tea and sweet cakes for his customers, with a view of the tranquil waterfall cascading down over moss-covered rocks into a pond, and there are many colorful koi visible swimming in and out from underneath the water lily pads.

The unique ambiance, of Mr. Ohara's establishment has lured many rich Americans; they come to see the one-of-its-kind precious gemstone jewelry, the diamonds, silver, gold, and pearls, and more which lured customers, some of them were just see inside of establishment.

"Come, Nana." I hear my little ones are calling me, and Yumi as always has prepared the hot tea and sweet cakes for us to enjoy

while viewing the sunset. Sitting with my family, my mind travels back in time to when I held Miss Tami on my lap, sitting next to Mistress Shizuka to watch the sunset from the verandah.

Sitting here in the comfort of my home, I reminisce over nostalgic memories in my private moments, recalling the times when we did not have any of life's necessities, often not even daily food even in our dreams we had no creature comforts. But the three of us girls made it through, relying only on our tenacity, intestinal fortitude, and strength. Ironically, I miss the camaraderie of those days, when strangers were not strangers, as we all helped one another trying to survive.

When in my solitude I often forget the passing time, and it is already dark. Yumi will come soon to help me into my bed, because I am no longer as steady on my feet as I used to be, and needs Yumi's steady arm. Ken has devised a button on my cane that works like a wireless doorbell; when I press it the buzzer sounds at their house, a measure of caution just in case of an emergency.

Before I close, I must tell you about Yumi's final embroidery she has made a life-size Oilan (geisha) existed centuries ago. It is being displayed at Mr. Ohara's antique shop. It was stitched with fine-colored silk fibers on unbleached hand-woven silk, and has a three-dimensional lifelike appearance. And the Oilan's eyes follows as you move, and often curios people would touch it, being mesmerized by her haunting beauty. So to protect it, Mr. Ohara has placed the Oilan in a glass case and illuminated the portrait with diffuse light, which created the Oilan's appearance yet more haunting. Many Americans as well as Japanese have offered unheard-of sums to buy it. But Mr. Ohara would not sell, no matter how large the offered sum was.

Those precious gems, which Mistress Shizuka had intended

for her daughter Miss Tami's future, has provided a second chance in life for many people she never knew.

I have come to an end of my story and faced with today's new technologies, which moving fast-forward into the new millennium, advancing to yet higher levels and the new generations were discovering the space-age techno-advancements. However, in my declining years, I cherish my precious memories of so long ago, when three of us were refugees, and Miss Tami, Yumi, and myself had to survive a moment-to-moment and day-to-day.

Ever since I received a package from Thomas, I have been thinking more about his offer of come to the US, and I am seriously considering accepting his invitation to find Miss Tami. Although what I have in my mind is a little farfetched, but there is a small chance of reaching Miss Tami, because I feel it in my heart I will find Miss Tami.

I have been mulling over my idea to appear on TV, asking viewing public for help, it's a small chance but someone must have seeing Miss Tami, or knew where she is. And I am offering $50.000 as a reward, for information. Yumi and I have applied for a passport; and I wrote a letter to Thomas explaining my idea his Nisei detective will translate my letter for him.

When Yumi and I have disembarked Plane at the LAX, Thomas was waiting for us at the gate, and so happy to see both of us, also he brought his detective friend to translate our conversation. We were driving through Los Angeles skyway just as Miss Tami did, and Yumi and I were awe struck to see huge cityscape as Miss Tami must have.

Following day I had an appointment at the local TV station, to tape my message, appeal to the viewers for a help. Immediately I prepare the note, along with Miss Tami's wedding photo, her engagement amethyst ring, and photo of Tenshi. I hoped all these photo will jog her mind and helps her to comes out of amnesia.

It has been four days my plea for finding Miss Tami was broadcasted, but no telephone call came. My Visa was for two weeks and Yumi and I have to leave in two days, we were getting our things packed for return trip. Thomas was just as heartbroken as I was, but just in case phone call would come after we leave, I am leaving reward money of $50.000 with Thomas and tip for his detective friend, who took his time to help us.

In an evening, four of us decided to go out for dinner, that's when a car drove up in a front of house, slender good looking woman stepped out and stood there looking at the house, hesitating to come and ring the doorbell. Even though there was change in her look, but I knew the woman had to be Miss Tami; we walked up to her, asked to come inside.

"My name is Cindy; I don't know what possessed me to come here?" She said. I was shaking seen Miss Tami in a front of me. Thomas asked her to come inside, four of us were sitting in a living room, and I can see that the Miss Tami was nervous; Thomas offered green tea she has enjoyed in a past.

"Anything looks familiar to you, Cindy?" Thomas asked and watched Miss Tami's reaction. But she showed no recognition.

Miss Tami stared at a large wedding portrait, and said,

"That my husband James and woman looks like me, where did you get it?" A minute she said that, I cannot hold back my thought any longer and said,

"Miss, your name is Tami Araki, and I am your servant Taka, My sister Yumi and I came from Japan to take you home."

Miss Tami looked Yumi and I as if to ply open a door all of her memories were locked inside, but as little as she has recalled gave me a hope of Miss Tami will comes back to us. Yumi and I have extended the visa for one more week, to have Miss Tami and us to get acquainted.

Morning of departure, we bid good-by to Thomas and detective friend, boarded 747 via Japan.

Miss Tami did not talk much, but she no longer had a fear of uncertainty on her expression. While in flight, I told all about her estate and waiting servants I saw a smile came on her face. I took her hand told her when she is well enough, we will visit Thomas and his detective friend.

An Afterthought

At the beginning of time, an erupting volcano created a mountain and a peninsula was born, it was named Unzen, the Sacred Cloud. The peninsula became known as Shimabara, a tropical paradise, Garden of Eden, and people were lured to the paradise, settled there and built their homesteads. People came from Europe as well, but they settled in Nagasaki, across the bay from Mount Unzen, and the European has introduced Christianity into the country of Buddhism and Shintoism, but surprisingly all have co- existed in harmony.

On August 9, 1945, an experimental atomic bomb was dropped on the bustling city of Nagasaki, and in a blink of an eye the explosion pulverized the city into an unrecognizable vast wasteland. Nothing remained as far as one's eyes could see, only a desert of ashes where the city and people had been a few moments before.

However, there was a torii—two stone columns supporting a curved lintel and a stone crossbar, which the people walked through to enter the shrine—that was sheared in half by the blast but one half was left undisturbed, supported by a tilted single torii column balancing precariously, as if it would tumble down at any minute.

To this day, half of the torii resembling an italic F is still standing defying the law of physics, carrying a half of curved lintel and stone crossbar still intact. Sixty-plus years later the city of Nagasaki has been rebuilt to its former being, but the half torii was kept in its original location as a memorial to the war that has changed course of the world.

On June 3, 1991, after two hundred years of dormancy, Mount Unzen erupted; spewing pyroclastic ashes buried the village of Shimabara. Among the victims were American volcanologist Henry Glicken, French volcanologists Murice and Katia Kroft, and forty Japanese journalists and photographers. They were there to witness and chronicle the eruption and photograph the sequence of events, but were overtaken by the pyroclastic ashes descended fast downhill, and entombed under the hot ashes that hardened into rock. Later some bodies were exhumed and given proper funerals; Murice and Katia Kroft were among them.